Linda – from your favorite FBI agent Ken Aldridge

About the Author:

Ken Aldridge grew up in Nebraska and served 24 years as a Special Agent with the FBI. After his service in Tennessee, Minnesota and North Dakota he retired and currently lives with his wife, Vicki, in Texas. They spend their summers in Minnesota. They have three children and six grandchildren.

In retirement Aldridge enjoys the challenging hobbies of golf and stamp collecting. He is a member of the Mid-Cities Stamp Club and active in the Dallas Chapter of the Society of Former Special Agents of the FBI. Aldridge currently serves as Treasurer of NOMADS, a national charity involved in the repair and rebuilding of churches, church camps, homes and homeless centers.

In 2010 he sat down and wrote his first crime novel, “Triage of Troubles.” His second novel, a sequel, “Enticing Evils,” came out in 2012. “In Murder’s Shadow,” he takes his readers back to Lake City, TX which is featured in both of his first two books.

Acknowledgement

This book would have never been written if it weren't for the encouragement and support of my wife, Vicki, my family, friends and others who read my first two books. Thank you, thank you. I also want to thank Vicki for her advice, perspective and editing assistance to help bring this book to fruition.

Dedication

This book is being dedicated to all those individuals who took the time to buy, read and seek me out to thank me and tell me they enjoyed reading my books. Many of these people I had not met, but now I like to consider them part of my extended family. Thank you, everyone.

ISBN-13:978-1490970523

"For the morning is to them like the shadow of death: For they know the terrors of the shadow of Death" Job 24:17

In Murder's Shadow

By Ken Aldridge

CHAPTER 1

It was a bright, sunny April day, but rather cool with temperatures in the low 50's. This was near normal weather for the time of the year for Silver Springs, Maryland; a suburb of Washington, D.C. The Nicola Family earlier that Sunday enjoyed a brunch at Mrs. Nicola's favorite eating spot, Margie's Diner. The family consisted of Dr. David Nicola, his wife Sarah, two sons and one daughter. Their oldest son, Alexander, better known as Alex to all his friends, was not with his family at brunch that day.

Alex was spending Saturday and Saturday night with his best friend from high school, Jimmy Smith, who lived several miles from the Nicola home. Both of them were doing some last minute preparations to receive one more Merit Badge needed for their Eagle Scout Awards. The badge they were working on was for Stamp Collecting. He and Jimmy were going to present their Russian Stamp Collections to Scout Leaders in hopes of getting the last badge they both needed.

Alex Nicola had been collecting stamps since he was about eight years old, when he inherited his grandfather's stamp collection. What he inherited was primarily a Russian collection and over the years he added numerous other Russian stamps and organized them in an album. It was his interest in stamp collecting that got Jimmy involved. Alex wanted someone he could trade stamps with and share his hobby. They attended several stamp shows and bourses in the Washington, D.C. area several times each year.

His father, Dr. David Nicola, was born in Russia and came to the United States to work on a Ph.D. in Biological Science at Harvard University. Upon completion of his studies and receiving his doctorate degree, he was offered temporary but renewable citizenship if he accepted a research position with the US Department of Agriculture, researching and studying anthrax. He accepted the offer and relocated to Silver Springs where the research lab was located. He fit in well with the other researchers and eventually was promoted to Assistant Director and had recently received his 20 year government service pin.

Dr. Nicola met one of the lab's stenographers, Sarah, shortly after starting his research there and within the year they were married. Alex was born one year later. His father signed his son's birth certificate, "Dr. Davidovich Nicolashevsky," his true Russian birth name of record, although US Immigration and Naturalization personnel allowed him to shorten it to David Nicola upon his arrival to the States to study at Harvard.

That Sunday afternoon, the family was watching, "The

Sound of Music," a movie they all agreed on at the movie rental store on the way home from their brunch. It was late afternoon and unbeknownst to the Nicola family, their house was being watched. Three grey-colored, four-door sedans of two men each were strategically located within eyesight of the Nicola home. The home sat on a three acre lot with many well-developed trees and shrubs.

A low, bass-like voice crackled on the cars radios. "Traffic report?" It was the voice of Boris Kerensky, assigned to the Russian Embassy in Washington, D.C. He held the official title of Director of Public Affairs. But unofficially he carried the rank of Major General and was in charge of all of the KGB's operations in the U.S. He answered directly and only to, Anton Pavlovich, Commander, KGB Operations Central, The Kremlin, Moscow, Russia.

Today however, he was not at the embassy. Kerensky was radioing from a sub floor room at an off-site location in a vacant warehouse building. The building was located in a run down and mostly abandoned commercial district a few blocks from the Potomac River. With him in the room was his personal body guard and former Russian military defensive tactics trainer, his driver and two other well-experienced agents in whom he had only the utmost trust.

Most of Kerensky's six years were spent developing Dr. David Nicola as a spy for the KGB, passing on anthrax research as it was being developed and discovered in the USDA laboratory. This was a high priority of the KGB to add to its growing arsenal of biological and chemical weapons.

Although he resisted when first approached, it didn't take the KGB handler, Piotr Blok, long to convince Dr. Nicola that if he didn't cooperate, two elderly aunts and an uncle still residing in Russia would be totally cut off from their meager, but yet life sustaining government pensions. Nicola finally relented and for several years passed on only the barest of information he thought he could get away with and so far it seemed to satisfy the Russians.

The primary goal for Dr. Nicola's research was actually to develop a vaccine for the US Military. This entailed studies and research of not only direct exposure to anthrax through open wounds or cuts but also exposure to anthrax spores, which when inhaled, lead to internal bleeding, swelling and tissue death.

A secret, special division of the USDA Lab, directly under Dr. Nicola's supervision, was also researching a high potency strain of anthrax that could be put into powder form. This strain when exposed to the open air, would lead to eventual, inevitable death. The Soviet's interest and the KGB's mission, was to come up with the formula and research data for development of the special strain anthrax powder.

The only contact he ever had with the Russians was with Piotr Blok, who on that Sunday afternoon, answered Kerensky's radio call, "Traffic clear."

"Proceed," was Kerensky's reply, meaning to go ahead with the operation. The Russians as well as the CIA and FBI all used radios that scrambled the signals, but the Soviets still limited the radio calls to the minimum of conversation, mostly out of old habits. The three cars immediately drove up to the Nicola home and all six men hastily exited their vehicles, two to the rear of the house and four to the front door. They all carried side arms and two of them had Israeli Uzi's.

The first man to the front door of the Nicola residence rammed his 6'5", 300 pound body into the solid wooden door and it immediately came off its hinges. The two at the rear, one with an Uzi, stood guard and attentive if anyone tried to exit out the back. The second agent through the front door carried an Uzi and was followed by Piotr Blok.

The Nicola family froze in their movie watching positions at the sound of the door crashing down. They never knew what hit them. Several bullets were targeted and fired into each of them. The silencer on the Uzi minimized the loud short bursts of gunfire. Agent Blok realized immediately Alex was not with the other family members all seated and now slumped and dead on the circular sofa. He motioned for the others to check the rest of the main floor rooms and waved for the agent with the Uzi to follow him upstairs.

A quick search of the rooms on the second floor revealed Alex was not there and after returning to the living room, the other Russians shook their heads, indicating no one else was home. The KGB Agents rushed out of the house and got into their cars. They drove swiftly to the street in front of the residence and left in opposite directions.

Piotr Blok picked up his radio. "Traffic stopped, one car missing," (killed, but one family member not there). There was nothing but silence on the air and no response for almost a minute.

Finally, Kerensky came on the air, "Return to garage" (the offsite command post). "Wham," Kerensky, with a scowl on his face, slammed his cane into the side of an old desk. He had to think of something and something fast. Anton Pavlovich, Commander of KGB Operations, would be expecting a secure telephone report on "Operation Traffic," within the hour.

CHAPTER 2

"Operation Traffic," was in the planning stages for several months. At first it was the information that Dr. Nicola was giving to Piotr Blok. It was becoming less significant and Nicola was becoming less available with more and more excuses in meeting with Blok.

Then there was the incident at the National Gallery of Art. Piotr Blok, planning to secretly meet with another coerced American scientist at the Gallery, happened to spot Dr. Nicola hand a newspaper to a well-dressed younger man. Blok quickly photographed the two together using his ball point pen camera as he appeared to be taking notes of some of the artwork.

Having photos, descriptions and addresses of all of the FBI personnel assigned to the Washington Field Office, commonly known as "WFO," as well as employees in the J. Edgar Hoover Building, had long been a necessity and a major priority of the KGB. Using data in the KGB's computer system didn't take them long to determine the man's identity. He was FBI Special Agent Willis Emerson II, assigned to the Foreign Counterintelligence Squad at WFO.

And there was a chance encounter one day when young Alex Nicola came upon his dad and Blok. Alex was on a field trip with his high school biology class. They were spending a half day at the National Arboretum learning what effect environment has on plant life. He saw his dad sitting at a picnic table drinking a cup of coffee. As he approached Dr. Nicola, he observed his father talking to a man. Alex didn't recognize the man and when he walked up to the table and looked at the man and then his father, his father had a very startled look on his face.

Dr. Nicola quickly got up from the table and walked Alex away from the other man. He asked his son what he was doing there. After he told his father about the field trip, his father told him he was meeting with one of the researchers at the Arboretum as a prospective employee of the USDA Lab. He told Alex he didn't have much time before the man had to go back to work and asked him to leave so they could finish the interview.

KGB Commander Pavlovich and his loyal confidants in Moscow wrestled with various solutions to neutralize Dr. Nicola and his relationship with the Russians. They were not worried about Dr. Nicola himself, since the Soviets still had the threat of cutting off pensions for his uncle and aunts. A slightly stickier problem was the potential the FBI had knowledge of Piotr Blok being a Russian spy. If so, they would now be on him like, "flies on shit," as long as he remained in Washington. He might have to be replaced and ordered back to Russia with a new assignment.

Then there was the boy, Alex Nicola. This was a major

concern for Pavlovich. The boy saw Blok with his father and probably by now figured out his father was a spy. He may be aware that his father was also working with the FBI. The problem was, how much more about his father's activities did he know and who might he tell?

If that wasn't enough, Soviets had already been struggling with how to respond to an assassination of one of their double agents in St. Petersburg, Russia earlier that year. It was an obvious hit by one of the US agencies, probably the CIA, and most likely at the request of the FBI.

The normal, Cold War reaction by both the Russian and American intelligence agencies to one of their own being exposed and sent back home was to have someone ripe and ready to also expose and send home. Sort of a "tit for tat," procedure or like a school yard retort, "Nana, nana, boo, boo." All of these factors weighed into the final decision by Pavlovich and his Board of Generals, to immediately implement, "Operation Traffic."

Alex Nicola was "no one's dummy." A straight "A"

student all through school, he earned almost one year in college credits even before his graduation, scheduled in just a few weeks. He had an IQ of 130 and could read, write and converse in Russian and Spanish. Alex applied for and was accepted with a "Full Ride Scholarship," at Cornell University, Ithaca, NY. He was planning on going there in the fall to study chemical and aeronautical engineering.

From an early age, Alex was a keen observer of people and their mannerisms. Sometimes he could actually sense what some of his classmates and friends were thinking, or about to do. Some of them often teased him and called him a, "Psycho." He didn't mind and actually enjoyed the idea that he was someone who might have a special gift.

Even before the chance meeting with his father and the strange man at the Arboretum, he had suspicions his father may be passing on some of his research to the CIA, FBI or to a foreign agency. There were a few times lately when it seemed his father was distracted or was worried about something. Dr. Nicola was now talking more and more about the importance of his research. He often made concerned comments after seeing something in the news or on television. Most of the coverage was about chemical warfare research and the growing interest of several foreign governments.

CHAPTER 3

A neighbor of the Nicola's, Rupe Walker, was working in his yard that Sunday afternoon. He was raking up leaves he missed in his fall leaf cleanup and burning. As he was bending over to pick up some of the raked up leaves, he thought he heard a slight squeal sound coming from the direction of the Nicola's home.

His hearing was not all that good anymore, but the sound did cause Walker to look up. Through the trees and shrubs between his house and the direction of the squeal sound, he caught a glimpse of two vehicles quickly pulling out of the Nicola's driveway and going in different directions. He didn't recognize the vehicles and thought it a bit strange, since one hardly ever even saw the Nicola's or heard much at all from their place. He decided to mention it to his wife, Ima, when he finished raking. She was in a monthly bridge group with Sarah Nicola and may know of a party or something going on at the Nicola's.

Ima Walker was not as close to Sarah Nicola as she was with some of the other neighbor ladies. She did see her on a monthly basis and enjoyed her and the other ladies in the card club. The Walkers invited the Nicola's to their house several times over the years, to a few special parties or celebrations, but the Nicolas always had a reason they couldn't make it. They were the quietest neighbors the Walkers ever had.

When her husband came in and mentioned the vehicles, Ima was a little surprised. She was fixing a kettle of chicken and noodles and had just put in the noodles. She sat down to a glass of chardonnay as her husband went to the refrigerator and got himself a bottle of beer.

Rupe Walker could talk about anything to anybody and was going on and on about the yard between sips of his beer. Ima was listening off and on, as she usually did, but for some reason couldn't stop thinking about what her husband said he heard and saw at the Nicola's.

She said to Rupe, "One of the cars wasn't Alex was it?"

He looked at her and said, "No, he drives a little white car doesn't he?"

She answered, "Yes. I think Sarah said he's been spending a lot of time with his friend Jimmy Smith. They're working on some kind of a scouting project." After a few more sips of her wine, Ima said to Rupe, "I'm going over to check on them."

"What?" he asked in a surprised tone.

"I'll be right back," and she walked out of the house.

Ima Walker cut through the back of their property and headed through the trees to the Nicola house. As she came around to the front, she saw the front door smashed in and she let out a gasp. She turned and ran back to her house. She ran for the phone and called the police as her husband watched with a bewildered look on his face.

After making the call, Ima, a little shaken by what she saw, sat down and told her husband about the broken down door. A couple of minutes later, they saw two police cars turn into the Nicola driveway and head toward the house. The Walkers left their house and headed for the Nicola's. They walked briskly, and Rupe had trouble keeping up with his wife. As they approached the front of the residence, they observed two police officers go through the front door, one headed to the rear and a fourth one was standing in front. He had a portable radio in one hand and a drawn revolver in the other. He motioned for the Walkers to stay back and they stopped in their tracks.

Ima Walker wanted to tell the officer she was the one that called the police and also about the two cars her husband, Rupe, observed. There was a cackle sound that came from the officer's radio. He responded but the Walkers were out of ear shot. Then another cackle over the radio and again the officer said something into the radio. He turned and walked over to the Walkers.

Ima Walker immediately identified herself and her husband and told the officer she was the one that called the police. "Are the Nicola's okay?" she asked.

The officer was taking out a small spiral pad from his top shirt pocket. "Not sure, just yet, ma'am. Officers inside are still checking. How well do you know the people who live here?"

"Well, we've been neighbors for a number of years but really don't see much of them. I play bridge with Mrs. Nicola every month. He works at the USDA Lab in town and they have two sons and a daughter."

The officer was jotting some notes as Mrs. Walker talked to him. He looked up and asked," Did you say two sons and a daughter?"

"Yes sir, I did."

Suddenly the sound of a siren could be heard far off in the distance. At the same time, one of the officers who had been inside, came out of the front door and motioned for the officer talking to the Walkers to come toward him. The two men huddled for a few moments and the one officer went back into the house. The officer returned to where he left the Walker's standing.

"Fraid I've got some bad news, folks. There's a man, woman, a boy and girl inside that appear to have been shot." Ima let out big gasp, with her hand coming up to cover her mouth.

"Oh no, that can't be," she said. Rupe Walker seemed to be in shock and just stared at the officer.

"Fraid so ma'am, they're all dead." The siren sounds were getting very loud now and an ambulance pulled into the drive. The wailing stopped as it headed toward the Walkers and the officer.

The officer turned back to Ima Walker. "You did say the family had two boys, is that right?"

"Yes, officer. There's Alex and Adam, Alex is the oldest and…." looking to the other side of the house, added, "I don't see Alex's car. It's a little white car. Oh, I remember now, I think he is staying with a friend this weekend." She gave him Jimmy Smith's name adding, "I think they live near the Catholic Church just off Chesapeake Boulevard."

By now EMT's were rushing out of the ambulance carrying various bags and equipment, and ran into the house. The officer turned back to the Walkers and after getting their phone number, address and full names, asked them to return to their house and they would be contacted a little later. He instructed them to not say anything to anyone about the matter.

On their walk back to their home, Ima Walker started sobbing. Rupe put his arm around her and said "Now, now Ima, it'll be all right." He pulled her tight to his side as they neared their house. Inside Rupe filled two cups with water and put them into the microwave. When they got hot, he added a little brandy to both cups and gave one to his wife, who was sobbing and muttering, "I can't believe it, I just can't believe it."

CHAPTER 4

Jimmy Smith, his parents and his friend Alex were in the process of devouring one of Mrs. Smith's homemade sausage pizzas when the doorbell rang. Mr. Smith opened his front door to two police officers, one male and one female. In quiet, serious tones they asked Mr. Smith if an Alex Nicola was there and after he told them he was, they asked to speak to him.

It was there, in the kitchen of the home of his best friend that Alexander Nicola learned of the shocking fate of his family. He looked from officer to officer as they continued on about the house being inaccessible for a couple of days, how the department was pursuing the investigation vigorously and some more words that seemed to just go and on, not all actually reaching Alex's ears. Mr. and Mrs. Smith each had an arm around his shoulders as they stood and listened to the officers. Jimmy Smith had his head in his hands and you could hear him softly uttering whimpering sobs.

Major General Boris Kerensky couldn't wait any longer to notify Commander Pavlovich of the results of "Operation Traffic." He discussed the situation with his men upon their return to the offsite warehouse location. He did not have many options or answers about locating the young Nicola boy. His only hope was that Pavlovich, by now, had partaken in his normal evening drinking routine. The routine of attacking a bottle of Stolichnaya vodka, thus allowing Kerensky to easily put "spin" on his gallant efforts to find and eliminate the boy.

He made the call. He reached Pavlovich at the Commander's dacha located on a lake about 100 kilometers north of Moscow. His wife, Hilda, passed out earlier that evening from her usual over indulgence of vodka and he had put her to bed. He was dozing in his favorite, overstuffed easy chair in the den of the dacha when the call came through.

He was alone in the dacha, except for his wife, snoring away in the bedroom. Four KGB Special Operations Agents were guarding the outside of the heavily wooded summer residence. He almost knocked over the empty bottle of Stolichnaya sitting next to the phone as he reached to answer it and stop the loud, sharp rings.

The conversation was actually rather brief and Boris did his best to make it sound like, "Operation Traffic," went off as planned except for locating the boy, Alex, who they were looking for as they spoke. He lied to the KGB Commander assuring him they would find the boy soon, since they had and were working on several good, solid leads. Kerensky had been in and out of various KGB divisions with numerous responsibilities over the years. He knew what worked and what didn't work and how far one could stretch the truth.

Boris Kerensky was a savvy student of maneuvering his cohorts with an uncanny ability to step on those he wanted out of the way and kiss up to those who could enhance his career. He knew his explanation to Pavlovich would not have been so readily accepted if the information had been relayed during regular working hours. And this time, he was right again, receiving only a few mumbles from Pavlovich to "Carry on," and teletype Moscow with daily updates.

Before they left the Smith's residence, the police told Alex one of their detectives would come by and talk to him in the morning. After they left, Mrs. Smith contacted a minister from the Methodist church they attended. He readily agreed to come right over. Although Alex and his family were Russian Orthodox, Alex sat and quietly listened to the man quote a few scriptures from the Bible and attempt to console the boy. After the minister left, Mrs. Smith told Alex he could stay with them, "For as long as you want or need to," and he nodded while uttering a subdued, "Thanks."

That night, as Alex Nicola lay awake in the lower bunk in Jimmy Smith's bedroom, a plan started to take form. He knew why his family had been murdered and strongly believed it was the Russians. They would now be looking for him. It was basically a plan of desperation, but the only logical one he could think of since he really had so few options.

The police would be back the next day. He could tell them everything he knew about his father and his secret contacts, or lie to them that he had no idea why his family had been murdered. If he told them everything he knew the police still couldn't protect him. If he lied and stayed with the Smith's for a while, that might put their lives in jeopardy. He knew of no one else he could stay with. He couldn't go live with one of his Russian aunts or uncles, which would put him right under the KGB's noses. No, Alexander Nicola had only one logical option.

After Major General Boris Kerensky hung up from the call to Pavlovich, he ordered everyone present in the warehouse to return to the embassy to immediately formulate plans and ideas on how to locate and eliminate Alex Nicola. In route to the embassy, he radioed the all-night dispatcher to contact the three embassy Data Analysts and have them proceed to his office within the hour.

As per usual embassy staffing, the analysts used cover titles somewhat justifying their presence on the staff. This was true for the Russians as well as the U.S. and many other countries. One was the Embassy Photographer, another had the title of Assistant Attaché of Social and Cultural Affairs and the third was listed as one of the chauffeurs. All three were KGB operatives, highly educated, screened and trained in computer science.

CHAPTER 5

Alex looked at the clock on the AM-FM radio sitting next to his bunk. It read, "2:15." He had not slept a wink. A slight glimmer of moon light came through a small gap in the drapes of one of the bedroom windows. He slowly sat up and looked around. Jimmy Smith's breathing was steady and he could hear a slight sound of air each time he inhaled.

He very quietly stood up and slipped on his pants and shirt. He picked up his shoes and socks and tip-toed over to a medium-height, wooden dresser. On top of the dresser were items Jimmy removed from his pants before taking them off and getting into bed.

Alex picked up Jimmy's billfold and the keys to his tan 1980 Olds Cutlass. As he started for the bedroom door, his eye caught sight of his Russian stamp album. He grabbed the album and then carefully opened the bedroom door. The door cooperated with no squeaks or other tell-tale sounds. He went through the doorway, slowly closed the door and headed for the front of the house. At the front door, he listened for any stirring. Everything was quiet.

Mr. and Mrs. Smith's bedroom was on the second floor of the home, located in the back, above but adjacent to Jimmy's bedroom. The front door bolt lock turned easily and the next thing he knew, he was hurrying toward Jimmy's car. Alex's only chance now was that the starting of the car did not disturb anyone. The Olds Cutlass started on the first turn of the key and he slowly backed it out of the driveway and headed west out of the Silver Springs area.

There were a total of ten, including Kerensky, present in the inner meeting room of the Russian Embassy. The building was ironically located on one of the higher elevations in the whole Washington, D.C. metro area. This was not by chance. The Soviet Union, using political force and diplomatic guile, was able to persuade the US State Department in locating the embassy at that location when the old one became too small and was starting to deteriorate. This gave them a great advantage in all their overt, as well as covert, communications and a challenge for the various US intelligence agencies.

The clock on the wall in the meeting room read 1:20 a.m. Some of those present were still a little hung over from a late night engagement party. A party for one of the young staffers and his girlfriend, Anna, who worked for the US Social Security Administration. The two of them meeting and starting to date, was not by chance, but rather a scheme set up and facilitated by the KGB.

Kerensky's personal secretary, Yakov, and his wife Maria, lived in a three story apartment building in the suburb of Alexandria, Virginia. One day, a young woman moved into their apartment building just down the hall from Yakov. When he and Maria welcomed her to the building, they learned her parents emigrated to America from Russia and she was employed as a clerk with the Social Security Administration.

When advised the next day of Yakov's new neighbor and her employer, Kerensky moved quickly, assigning Yakov and two of the most trusted operatives to covertly arrange a meeting between Anna and one of the embassy's young single staffers. That was six months ago and the scheme to put the couple together worked out just as planned.

CHAPTER 6

About the time the Russians were starting their meeting to set plans to locate and eliminate Alex Nicola, he was turning off Interstate 95 onto Interstate 64 heading west. As the car rounded just above a deep ravine, Alex removed the bills from his wallet and tossed it out the window into the ravine. He had not taken time to even count how much money he had or think where was going. He thought he had about $50 but did not know how much was in Jimmy's billfold. He only knew he had to get as far away from Washington, D.C. as fast as he could.

He glanced at the Oldsmobile's gas gauge. It showed a

little less than half a tank. As he proceeded west he began to think about getting used to his new identity, James Alan Smith, aka Jimmy. His earlier sleeplessness gave him time to plan the stealing of Jimmy's car, his billfold and his identity. They were both about the same height and weight, with fairly similar facial features. Jimmy wore glasses so Alex would have to pick up a cheap pair of reading glasses as soon as possible. He spotted a rest area sign but continued driving, afraid he was still not far enough away from the metro area and someone might recognize him.

Alexander Nicola was almost six foot tall and with a muscular, athletic build. He was not involved in any athletics in high school, although he did play on soccer teams until entering high school. His high school days were focused on academics and that also precluded much attention to the fairer sex. He had dark brown eyes and a slightly predominant chin. He also had to start shaving at an early age and now by most afternoons, had a "five o'clock shadow." Most people who didn't know him thought of him as several years older than his actual age.

Major General Kerensky, a short, stoutly built man with a distinctive pinkish complexion, was in his early 50's. He was prone to sweating easily and wore a toupee everywhere he went, taking it off before he went to bed. His premature baldness was an affront to him and at the earliest stages of hair loss he got fitted for a wig by one of Moscow's foremost wig makers. Now at the meeting he was conducting with his staff, he was getting more and more upset. Physically shaking his arms and fists as he talked, his complexion turned to dark pink and the wig somehow became slightly turned.

The turned wig was now so noticeable that every one of the staff present, even Kerensky's most trusted employees, could not take their eyes off it. Some were wondering if it was going to turn more, some wondered if it would turn back into place and others thought it might just fall off. A couple of the staffers had to look away in an effort to hold back grins. After laying out his demands to his staff, he wiped his sweating brow with a handkerchief. Looking around the room, person to person, he told them he wanted ideas and he wanted them now.

Kerensky was a hard-working, dedicated employee of the KGB. He had a near perfect record and received nearly the highest ratings as he worked his way up the chain of command. Single and never married, everyone believed he was married to the job and probably even spent his off hours doing paperwork, going over files or planning the daily course of business of the embassy. Little did they know, however, that he was not perfect and not totally dedicated to his job. Some of those off-hours activities were arranged by his secretary, Yakov, for Kerensky to be with prostitutes.

Alex was getting a little low on gas and he had to take a pee. He saw billboard signs of a Flying J Truck Stop at the exit on Interstate 64 onto Interstate 81. When he saw the gas station's tall sign outside the station, he took the frontage road exit. He pulled up to a gas pump and then removed Jimmy's billfold from his back pants pocket. He counted the money. There were 65 dollars. He pulled the bills he earlier put in his front pocket. He had 55 dollars, for a total of 120 dollars.

He entered the station and gave the attendant 10 dollars to prepay for the gas. After he put in the gas, he pulled the car around the corner behind the station and went back in to use the restroom. On his way out he bought a tuna salad sandwich, a Dr. Pepper and a set of cheap reading glasses. He got back into the tan Cutlass and headed back onto Interstate 81. He ate his sandwich and drank the Dr. Pepper as he drove.

CHAPTER 7

The KGB meeting was going well. Several ideas were brought up and as Kerensky turned from one of the people speaking to another, somehow his wig got turned back to its original place. As far as the staffers knew, the Nicola's had no close relatives, at least in the Washington, D.C. area. Someone suggested trying to identify some of Alex's friends. This led to several avenues to take to try to identify who they might be. After several hours of ideas and suggestions, only two were agreed upon.

The first idea was canvasing the Nicola neighborhood. Soviet agents would pose as fellow employees at the

Doctor's lab, soliciting funds for a family memorial. The second was secretly photographing people at the Nicola's funeral. The door to door idea would give the callers an opportunity to perhaps ask about young Alex, his whereabouts or getting names of some of his friends. Photographs at the funeral might help identify some of his friends and classmates.

Yakov and Maria's neighbor, who the KGB targeted as a person of interest and one who could possibly be coerced or pressured to obtain information from the files of the Social Security Administration, was Anna Bukhart. Anna was a basically shy, 23 year old with a slender build, but large breasts. She wore her dark blonde hair short and had a very fair complexion. Her lips were thinner than most girls her age, and she tried to compensate by wearing a lot of lipstick. Bright red was her color of choice. Anna had fairly thick dark eyebrows which caused for an unusual contrast with her fair complexion and abundantly layered lipstick.

She was the only child of Mr. and Mrs. Andrev

Bukhart, who were college professors at a small state college, outside of Baltimore, Maryland. Anna's great grandfather was Mikhail Bukharin, who was among some of the first former Russian military officers to be trained in security and intelligence for the Russian Government soon after WWI.

The intelligence service that now included the secret police, in 1954 was named the KGB, or Committee for State Security. Anna's grandfather was born not knowing his father, who was accidently shot during a firearms training exercise. The family left Russia just before World War II broke out, relocating in Finland and eventually gaining passage to the United States. When her grandfather registered with immigration officials the name Bukharin became Bukhart as a result of her grandfather's heavy accent and a misunderstanding by the Immigration official handling his papers.

Anna was an average high school student. She was in few extracurricular activities, mostly school plays and Drama Club. She only had a handful of casual acquaintances during her high school years. She would be the person few people would later recall, even looking at her picture in yearbook photos. After graduation, she enrolled in the state college where her parents taught. She started out in Theater Arts courses, but after two years, she lost, or perhaps never had, the enthusiasm to continue and she started looking for a job. Her parents were able to arrange for a college internship program with the Social Security Administration office in Baltimore by falsifying her educational goals.

. After almost a year in Baltimore, Anna put in for and was accepted for an opening in the Social Security Office in Washington, D.C. as a GS-3 file clerk. Her parents helped her find the apartment that was down the hall from Yakov and Maria. It was in this building where Anna first met Gagari Putin, a KGB analyst at the Russian Embassy.

Gagari was 24 years old, had slicked back black hair, a lanky build and a friendly smile. Let's just say he was a charmer who got the attention of all the females at the embassy, as well as at most other places he frequented. He was selected by Kerensky and his secretary, Yakov, to be the one to establish a friendship with Anna Bukhart.

At first, Gagari did not like the idea at all. Kerensky lied to him, stating it was an order that came out of Moscow. He also promised Gagari he'd be up for promotion as well as recommended for a medal if he could win Anna over and gain access to the files in her office. That incentive along with seeing surveillance photos of Anna and her curvy figure was finally enough to convince young Gagari to pursue a relationship with her.

That was about six months earlier and it all started at a party in Yakov's apartment where Anna Bukhart and Gagari Putin met for the first time. That meeting and the relationship that followed would become the bane of Alex Nicola's efforts to survive and lead a normal life as James Alan Smith.

CHAPTER 8

Kerensky and his KGB cohorts decided to wait for two days before sending people out to canvass the Nicola family's neighborhood. Any earlier and people could get suspicious. Agents going to do the canvassing were issued fraudulent ID's just in case someone might ask for some identification. The Russian Embassy had a photo lab and an excellent print shop located in the basement. Fake ID's were something they worked with almost on a weekly basis.

Alex reached Beckley, West Virginia around six a.m. He was tired and thought about getting a motel, but it was too early, so he drove around Beckley until he found a Wal-Mart Store. He parked off to one side but near several other cars, probably belonging to employees. He made sure the doors were locked and then he leaned back and closed his eyes. He thought about calling Jimmy, but decided against it. Besides, he knew Alex took his billfold and car, so what could he say?

This made Alex think about the car. There would be an APB put out on Jimmy's Oldsmobile Cutlass. He couldn't keep driving it for too long. He got out and looked at the car parked next to him. It had West Virginia tags and he decided if he stayed in West Virginia for a while he'd better have plates from that state. He looked around. It was still early and not much traffic at all. He remembered Jimmy had an emergency kit in his trunk. Alex got out of the car and opened the trunk. The kit contained a screwdriver and he used it to trade license plates with an older blue Buick.

When he finished, he got back into the Olds, left the Wal-Mart parking lot and started looking for a truck stop. A few minutes later, heading back toward the interstate, he found a small truck stop on the right side of the road. He pulled around to the rear of the parking lot and found an open parking spot among several vehicles he assumed belonged to truck stop employees. Alex Nicola leaned back and quickly fell asleep.

After the embassy meeting, Kerensky motioned for his secretary to stay while the others left the room. When the room was empty, he told Yakov he needed another date, which Yakov knew meant he wanted him to line up another prostitute.

"When," asked Yakov.

"Noon," he answered, "usual place and this time I want two."

"Two?" questioned Yakov.

"Da, dva." (Yes, two).

The next day's edition of the Washington Post as well as several of the suburbs papers carried various stories and theories of the murder of the Nicola family. Several of the stories showed street photos of the Nicola house, but the Post also ran a photo of Dr. David Nicola they obtained through their contacts with the Anthrax Research Laboratory.

Police media contacts gave out little information. They identified the victims and the approximate time of the crime. They also reported that a son was staying with a friend and not a home at the time of the shooting. The police also refused to speculate as to the motive of the killings and asked for help from the public if anyone had any information or saw anyone or cars at or near the house at the time of the murder.

Homicide detectives from the District of Columbia Police Department and from the Silver Springs Police Department met early the next morning at a conference room at the Silver Springs Police Department to plan a coordinated investigation. The general consensus from information gathered thus far, with no evidence of robbery, led them to believe the murders had something to do with Dr. Nicola's position and research at the U.S. Department of Agriculture's Anthrax Research Laboratory.

CHAPTER 9

The Mayflower Hotel was one of Washington, D.C.'s oldest and finest hotels. It was located just a few blocks from some of the most important U.S. Government offices and buildings in the district. Many dignitaries, congressional people and government staff frequented the hotel, mostly for its outstanding dining.

One of the officials, now deceased, who used to frequent the hotel for lunch was the director of the FBI, J. Edgar Hoover. The FBI still had a presence at the Mayflower, secretly filming the sexual exploits of Kerensky and taping covert meetings with Russian officials.

Information from the filming and taping for intelligence purposes was for possible dissemination to the White House. It was stored away until possibly needed in any future public disclosures and deportations of spies between the agencies.

The desk clerk recognized Kerensky as he approached the hotels check-in counter. The clerk reached for and gave him the room key as he arrived at the counter. The room was already paid for and was one the Russian Embassy used from time to time to entertain, house Russian officials and for Kerensky's trysts.

When he opened the door to room 231, he smelled the odor of lavender, his favorite and an odor that for some unknown reason always turned him on. The smell of the lavender and seeing three iced down bottles of champagne next to the oversized bed, made him chuckle and he made a mental note to submit Yakov's name for the monthly embassy employee of the month award.

As Kerensky was opening a bottle of champagne, he heard a soft knock on the door. He felt a slight twinge in his pants and with full anticipation quickly opened the door. Two beautiful, slim African-American women slowly entered the room. One, he knew from a previous sexual encounter, the other, he didn't know. He greeted them with a nod and a smile like one might see on a kid who was about to eat a double dip, chocolate chip ice cream cone.

Alex awoke with a start to the sound of a car starting up next to the Cutlass. He looked up and saw a young man, not paying any attention to Alex, slowly back up and drive away. He looked at his watch. It was shortly after 12 noon and he suddenly felt hunger pains. Since he was already at the truck stop he decided to go inside and get something to eat.

The menu was pretty basic with mostly sandwiches but they did have a luncheon special of a hamburger, French fries and drink for $3.99. He ordered the special with a Dr. Pepper. After the waitress turned and headed for the kitchen with his order, Alex looked around the café. Most customers appeared to be truck drivers and maybe a few construction workers.

Seeing the sign for the restroom, he headed that way. After relieving himself and as he started to walk back to the stool at the counter, he saw some notices pinned on a large bulletin board. He stopped and started glancing from notice to notice. Listings included auctions, people wanting babysitting or house cleaning jobs, items for sale, pictures of missing pets, etc. He started to turn away when his eye caught an ad, "Help Wanted."

He read the ad. It said the Friendship Mining Company was hiring drivers to pick up and take workers to their mine located ten miles north of the city. Alex found a napkin and borrowed a pen from the waitress as she set his order on the counter. He wrote down the phone number and address of where to apply.

CHAPTER 10

Special Agent Willis Emerson II and the Supervisor of the Foreign Intelligence Squad at WFO were also concerned about the whereabouts of young Alex Nicola. They were also worried about his safety. They knew why Dr. Nicola and his family were murdered, but weren't sure why the Nicola boy fled the area. They speculated it could have some connection to the killing of his family, and he may also have been sought by the KGB.

At a meeting Emerson had with his supervisor and several other squad members, a decision was made to keep a file open on Alex Nicola. The thinking was, if the KGB was interested in him, they could lead the Feds to the boy, whom local law enforcement still wanted to interview. They also thought if the boy's life was in danger, they may be in a position to come to his aid. An additional factor was the continuing efforts to monitor and study various Soviet intelligence gathering techniques. Agent Emerson and Agent Joseph Brewer were assigned to locating Alex Nicola. Their other cases were reassigned to other investigators so they could work the case full time.

After getting the information about the job with the Friendship Mining Company, he sat down and ate his hamburger. When he was almost finished, he got directions from the waitress and left the café headed for the mine office. He knew he needed money to keep on the run and would have to get a job as soon as possible. If he got the job he'd have to worry about a place to stay later. First things first, he thought.

Alex was a little surprised at the offices of the Friendship Mining Company. They were housed in a brick complex surrounded by nice trees and shrubs. The parking lot was mostly full but he had no trouble finding a spot in the second row from the front of the main building with a large sign that read: "Friendship Mining Company, A Company That Cares."

Upon entering the building he approached the receptionist sitting behind a small but neat desk. The girl behind the desk was very plain looking and the type he thought was probably a local high school drop-out who was happy to just have a job. She greeted him with a smile.

"May I help you?" she said.

"Ah, a, yes," said Alex. "I'm here about the driving position?"

The girl reached to one side of her desk and from a small stack of papers, handed him an application, adding, "Here you go."

"Thanks," he replied, glancing at her plastic name tag that said, "Mary." She was still smiling and looking at him. He found her smile somewhat infectious and returned the smile and a nod, before turning and heading to one of the chairs in the waiting area.

He took a seat and pushed up the reading glasses that had slipped slightly on his nose. He looked around the reception room before putting his attention to the application papers. There were three other males busy filling out papers, apparently also looking for a job. Alex, using Jimmy Smith's name and personal data, filled out the application. Under "Position Applying For," he put a check mark on "Any Available Position." The other applicants each returned to the receptionist desk in a slow procession.

Alex wondered if they all came together looking for work. He heard the girl mumble something to each one as she took the papers the men handed to her. Each returned to their seat, awaiting further instructions. He completed the application form and went back to Mary's desk.

"Please have a seat and someone will be with you shortly," she said in an encouraging tone.

"Thanks" replied Alex and he lingered at her desk for a moment.

"Did you have a question?" she asked as she studied his face.

"Oh, a, no, a, I mean not really," and he returned to his seat with her still staring at him.

He was watching Mary with a fascination and his thinking there was something about her that intrigued him. Alex wondered what was going on. He had hardly noticed any girls all through high school. *Why now? Why this girl?*

Then another girl sauntered into the reception area and retrieved some papers. Within a few minutes she returned and called out a name. One of the men got up and followed her into another room. This happened again about ten minutes later as the first guy came back out of the other room. Finally he heard, "Jimmy Smith," and he stood up and proceeded toward the girl who announced his name.

Through the door was a large open room with approximately 30 employees busy at their work stations. On both sides of the room were several small glass-partitioned offices. One was where the girl ahead of him was obviously leading him.

She opened the door to an office with, "Personnel Manager," in large red letters on the door and motioned for him to enter. A middle aged man dressed in a thin, blue striped suit stood up behind the desk where he had been sitting. He reached out his hand and announced his name. Alex shook his hand and the man pointed to a leather chair and said, "Have a seat."

The mining company needed drivers for various shifts to haul miners from the back office parking lot to their current working mine, about ten miles north of town. They urgently needed someone for the midnight to 8 a.m. shift and the man told him if he was interested he could start the next day. Alex just sat and listened, this being his first job application and first offer to go to work immediately.

"Well," the man said, "are you interested?"

Alex quickly said, "Yes, I am."

"Good," the manager replied. "It pays $5.65 per hour for an eight hour shift, five days a week and includes health insurance. It's not a union job so there are no union dues."

Alex was staring at the man. Finally he came to his senses and realized the man was still talking. "...see the girl that brought you in here and she'll give you the details about the job and where the employees park." The manager was at his door and ushered him out of his office, pointing to a desk where he saw the same girl who directed him to the man's office.

After going over the job details and benefits she told him he could start the next day. He had left the address space blank and told the girl he needed to find a place to stay. She told him her grandmother ran a boarding house and recommended he check with her. She wrote down the address and handed it to him.

CHAPTER 11

He found the boarding house located on a side street about four blocks from downtown Beckley. The landlady greeted him in her apron. She had light gray hair she wore in a bun on top of her head. Her body could be best described as "plump," and reminded Alex of Aunt Bea from the old "Andy Griffin Show." She was very cordial and showed him one of her upstairs rooms. She told him the rent was $300 a month and included meals and all utilities.

The room was clean with just a few pieces of furniture,

but he didn't need much. He told her he was just hired at the Friendship Mining Company and would take the room if he could give her $20 now, and the rest after he got his first paycheck. She told him that would be fine.

The room was a fairly large room. It had a twin size bed, a small desk and chair, and an overstuffed chair that sat beside a floor lamp. There was a small closet in one corner and next to it was a small sink. There was a window overlooking a side street and some houses. She told him the bathroom and shower were at the end of the hall and he'd have to share them with three other men, also mine employees who worked various shifts.

Alex asked the lady about a thrift store and she gave him direction to a Goodwill Store within walking distance. She handed him two keys and showed him which one was for the front entryway door and the other being his room key. He thanked her as she left the room, closing the door behind her. He turned the lock latch on the apartment door and laid down to catch up on some sleep. After a couple of hours, he checked the alarm clock on the bedside table and headed out the door for the Goodwill Store.

Since it was a fairly nice, sunny day, Alex decided to walk to the store. He found plenty of clothes his size to choose from and ended up buying three extra sets of everything, plus an extra pair of shoes and a navy colored knit hat. He thought the knit hat would be good for the cool night shifts and he planned to wear it anytime he left the apartment. As he walked back to the apartment he considered his current situation.

He had a job, a place to stay and food. He was worried about two things; Jimmy's Cutlass, which had stolen plates on it and the other car with Jimmy Smith's plates. If either plate would happen to be checked by the police, his efforts to disappear and lay low would be in jeopardy. His other main concern was his appearance.

He was already wearing the knit hat and the cheap pair of reading glasses he bought at the truck stop. If he let his facial hair grow, maybe he could groom it into a beard. Alex always wore his hair cut rather short, all through high school. Now he thought he'd let it grow long, helping with his disguise, as well as saving hair cut money. He concluded he would have to do something about the car, and do it fairly soon.

As Alex turned the corner, heading back to the boarding house, he saw some older cars parked in a row on a lot adjacent to the sidewalk. A weathered sign on a small shack at the rear of the lot read, "Lefty's Used Cars." He spotted an over-weight, middle-aged gentlemen wearing suspenders. The suspenders were pulling his pants about five inches off the ground and he had on red socks. Alex chuckled to himself. The man was standing next to one of the cars, talking to a young couple.

Alex's pace slowed and he stopped to look at the office sign. Below the main lettering it read, "We Finance," and below that was, "Insurance Available." A slight smile came on his face and he started walking again. He had a plan but would have to come back tomorrow and talk with the salesman, who was probably, "Lefty."

CHAPTER 12

When Alex reported for work at the mine's main office he found out there were two other drivers besides himself for his shift. They would be taking miners back and forth to the mine in old but refurbished school buses. Between the miner's shifts, he would be driving an eight passenger van taking various other employees, supervisors and occasional medical people back and forth.

The first night's shift went well and he was pleased with his ability to find a job so quickly. As he drove back to his apartment, the sun was starting to rise on the horizon. He thought after he had the boarding house breakfast and some sleep, he'd pay a visit to the used car lot he spotted the day before.

The KGB laboratory in the basement of the embassy was busy at work. With the high school photo of Alexander Nicola, they had already started putting various wigs, hats, eyeglasses and facial hair to the photo and were printing out possible disguises. Little did they know, that the FBI Laboratory's, Special Effects Division, right there in Washington, was busy doing the very same thing.

In addition, the neighborhood canvassing soliciting memorial funds for the Nicola family had started and already the KGB picked up information that Alex's best friend was Jimmy Smith. Alex had not been seen for several days and Jimmy's car and billfold were missing.

KGB Major General Boris Kerensky called an emergency meeting of his entire staff at the embassy. Now that they had an inkling Alex Nicola had taken off with Jimmy Smith's car and may be using Smith's name, he made specific assignments to contact the KGB informant who worked in the Washington, D.C. office of Motor Vehicles.

He also gave out orders to cover the Nicola funeral in case Alex might show up. Gagari Putin was to have his fiancée, Anna Bukhart, start checking Social Security records for any employment information in the names of Alexander Nicola or James Alan Smith. Kerensky also ordered his technicians to install a tap on Jimmy Smith's parent's telephone and tape all calls coming into or going out of the home.

This procedure was, of course, illegal and in violation of State Department Rules and Regulations agreements between the American and Russian Embassies. However, there was nothing in this agreement that said anything about Soviets tapping their citizen's lines in Russia or Americans tapping US citizen's lines in the U.S. This too, would have been illegal, at least for the US Government, if it hadn't been for a little known Presidential Order, first signed by President Harry S. Truman, oddly named, "The Emergency Enemies of the State Act."

This order, known only by the President, Vice-President, Secretary of State, and directors of the CIA and FBI, had been reissued by every succeeding president since Truman. The order included several very detailed actions that could be taken only under emergency and exigent circumstances. This included giving carte blanche authority for either the CIA or FBI to tap a US citizen's phone but only when in agreement between the President and the director of the agency requesting such authority.

This was the authority the FBI used to tap Jimmy Smith's parent's home telephone, which of course neither the FBI nor Russians knew the other was doing. Not like the Russians, who reviewed tapes every few hours, the FBI monitored the tap 24 hours a day. They had an advantage over the Soviets, knowing Jimmy Smith's driver's license, Social Security card and car had been stolen. The FBI proceeded with the belief there was a strong possibility Alex would use Jimmy's name and identity.

Another investigative avenue the FBI pursued was to request a "Mail Cover." This had to have approval of the

Special Agent in Charge of the requesting office. The request went to, and had to be approved by, the Chief Postal Inspector covering the address of the requested search. The search consisted of basically a stop placed on all mail being delivered to a specific person or address. In this case, it was the Smith's address. Mail personnel would record the return address information, date and location the piece was posted and date received at the destination post office before it was delivered as addressed. The Feds hoped, of course, Alex would send a letter to Jimmy. If he did, it could be a lead as to his location.

The funeral for the Nicola family was held at St. Peters Russian Orthodox church, in Silver Springs, Maryland. Burial was in the church's cemetery, located adjacent to the church. KGB and the FBI personnel were discreetly present looking for young Alex, but also secretly filming as many attendees as possible.

CHAPTER 13

Alex awoke at 3:50 p.m. He sat up and then remembered he wanted to check out the cars on Lefty's lot before it closed. He took a quick shower in the bathroom down the hall and put on some of the clothes he obtained from the Goodwill store. He'd bought mostly shirts and pants for work, but also found a couple of golf shirts and khaki slacks. He headed out the door and down the street to Lefty's.

The hefty salesman he saw the day before was puffing on a fat cigar and directing an apparent sales pitch to a middle-aged couple standing by an older black Buick. When Alex walked into the lot and between some cars, the salesman looked his way and nodded with a louder than normal, "Be right with you."

After a few minutes, he heard the man the salesman was talking to, say something about, "…thinking about it and maybe they'd come back the next day." Alex already spotted an early 70's Chevy Impala that had, "$900," written in white marker on the windshield. It had a few hardly noticeable dents and seemed to be pretty clean inside and out. The salesman walked up to him and said, "This is a dandy of a car, one of the best on my lot, young man," and as he was talking extended his hand for a handshake.

Alex shook his hand and the man said, "Lefty's the name, good deals is my game," and the man let out a deep, bass-toned laugh.

Alex replied, "Nice to meet you, I'm, ah, Jimmy, Jimmy Smith."

Lefty got into the Chevy and started it up. It started

immediately and seemed to run rather smoothly, at least it wasn't sputtering and no black smoke came out of the exhaust. Lefty got back out of the car and raised the hood. Alex didn't know what to look for under the hood, but pretended he did and just nodded his head as he looked the engine over.

Lefty was a veteran of car sales from way back. He could see he had an imminent sale and since business had been a little slow that month, told Alex he could let the car go for $800, if he bought it that day. He asked about financing and told Lefty he only had $20 he could put down on the car but had a new job at the Friendship Mining Company.

The salesman took out a piece of paper and a pen. He did some figuring and then told Alex with the $20 down, he could finance the car for nine months at $125 a month, including license and insurance. Alex agreed and Lefty invited him into his small office to sign papers. About 30 minutes later, he drove the 1972 Chevy Impala off the lot and headed out of town for a spin. He particularly wanted to find a place he could abandon Jimmy's Cutlass so it would never be found.

As Alex was leaving the outskirts of Beckley, he saw a sign, "Little Beaver State Park," and he turned south on that road. The area was heavily wooded and he could see some deep ravines on both sides of the road as he proceeded toward the park. He only drove a few miles from the city limits and he knew now what he had to do, and where, so he turned into a driveway and backing out, headed back to town. It was getting time for the evening dinner at the boarding house, which he didn't want to miss.

There were only four people at the dinner including the landlord and Alex. The two others were mine workers who worked the 8 a.m. to 4 p.m. shift. They both smelled heavily of beer and were more interested in diving into the platter of fried chicken than talking to or learning about Alex, which was fine with him. The chicken was crispy and delicious. They also had mashed potatoes, gravy, green beans, biscuits and peach cobbler. Alex stuffed himself and enjoyed every bite. He thanked the landlady, who seemed pleased at the hearty appetites and compliments from not only Alex but also from the other two tenants.

The sun was setting in the west when Alex exited the boarding house. It was still light enough for him to find his way back to the road to Little Beaver State Park. He headed for Jimmy's Oldsmobile Cutlass and then out the road to the park. He found a sharp drop off he had not seen earlier. Looking in front and to the rear, he saw no cars. He put the Olds in neutral and got out. It pushed easier than he thought it would and the next thing he knew the car went over the drop off and fell about a hundred yards into the deep, bushy ravine. Alex looked around, still no one coming or going on the road. He walked over and looked down at the car. He could barely see the left back fender and then only by leaning as far over the edge as he dared.

Satisfied with the abandonment of the Olds, he started walking back toward town. He had gone about a half mile when a car approached him from the rear. The driver slowed down and rolled down his window as he got next to Alex.

"Need a ride?" the man asked. He looked like a traveling salesman because he was wearing a suit and tie and Alex could see some boxes on the rear seat.

"No, thanks," he replied, "just getting a little exercise."

The man nodded, and as he drove on, Alex wondered if the man saw him ditch the Oldsmobile in the ravine. He surely would have said something if he had, and Alex continued walking.

On his way back into town, Alex's spirits lifted and he started to whistle in tune with his steps. He felt pretty good about taking care of his main problem, Jimmy's Oldsmobile. He had a job, a car and a nice room. He decided he would now concentrate on saving a little money and maybe even ask Mary out on a date. Nothing in these thoughts occurred to him that he may have to soon leave Beckley, West Virginia.

CHAPTER 14

The day after Alex pushed Jimmy's 1980 Oldsmobile over the cliff outside of town, the FBI alerted all 50 state Motor Vehicle Departments to put a stop on any re-registration of Jimmy's car as well as any new vehicle registrations in the name of James Alan Smith, or Alex Nicola. Driver's License Bureau records indicated Jimmy's license was only six months old and would not expire for another 18 months. Alexander Nicola's license wasn't due for renewal for another 15 months. Also on that same day, the FBI sent a request to all of the state's Driver's License Bureaus to notify the nearest office of the FBI if any effort was made to renew or reissue a license in the name of James Alan Smith or Alexander Nicola.

Mable Doolittle was a processing clerk for the State of West Virginia Department of Motor Vehicles, State Capitol Building, Charleston, WV. She worked in the department long enough to know that the more work you did, the more they expected you to do and it didn't get you any more money, accolades or promotions. In short, she had become a typical bureaucrat.

Oh, Doolittle knew how to keep enough paper flowing to not draw any attention to her performance. She spent a bigger portion of her day on the phone to her mother, either one of two sisters and conducting personal business. Besides, she and the other women in her office liked to spend a lot of the day visiting, discussing their husbands or boyfriends, personal problems, places to have lunch, shop, etc., etc. Five days after Alex made the deal with Lefty for the 1972 Impala; the paperwork from Lefty was dropped off on Doolittle's desk. She put it at the bottom of a pile of other applications about six inches thick.

The next six weeks went well for Alex. He was able to put a little money aside from each week's paycheck, hiding it in a plastic bag he taped to the back of the bed's headboard. He hadn't opened a checking account, paying his landlady and Lefty in cash. He still hadn't received his car registration. He did have the Bill of Sale and in West Virginia the plates stay with the vehicle. So, he really wasn't concerned about the delay.

His beard had reached the point where he needed to trim it a few times a week. He trimmed his long dark brown hair only once since arriving in Beckley. Alex got familiar with the city by running errands and frequenting his favorite book store. One day, after he returned to his room, it occurred to him that at no time did he feel like anyone was following him or did he see anything suspicious while he was out.

Mary was starting to greet him with a smile on more and more mornings after his shift ended. He made it a point to stop and chat with her if she was not busy. She was not wearing any engagement or wedding rings and he noticed she only wore a small silver chained necklace with a small cross. One day, he finally got up enough nerve to ask if she wanted to go with him to a movie and she readily accepted.

The date went well and the movie was one up for an Academy award. Later, over cokes, she did ask him about his family and he just told her they lived in Maryland, and let it go at that. He told her he wanted to eventually work his way to California and become an actor. Most of the conversation, Mary talked about her family and what it was like growing up in Beckley. He studied her face as she talked and was starting to have feelings for her. He asked her if she would like to go again sometime, and she said, "Yes, that would be nice."

While Alex was out and about in Beckley, he purposefully kept a low-profile. He was getting to know the other boarding house tenants, but always had an excuse to turn down invitations and other offers to hit the bars or party with them.

About three weeks later, a call was received at the Charleston Office of the FBI. It was from the West Virginia Department of Motor Vehicles. A supervisor from that office asked the FBI Agent about the alert from FBI Headquarters in Washington. The agent said he was aware of the alert. Then the man advised he just processed a vehicle registration for a James Alan Smith of Beckley, WV for a 1972 Chevrolet Impala.

The agent got the address and license number on the registration and thanked the official for the information. It would be another week before the same information was made available to the KGB from their informant in the Washington, D.C. Department of Motor Vehicles.

When the vehicle registration information was telephoned to WFO from the Charleston Resident Agency, it was given to the Foreign Intelligence Squad Supervisor, who summoned Special Agent Willis Emerson III into his office. Emerson was told of the vehicle registration information and to team up with Agent Joe Brewer and leave as soon as possible for Beckley, West Virginia.

Their instructions were to locate and conduct a surveillance of Alex Nicola. If it appeared he was being followed or approached by the KGB, they were to make themselves known to Alex, interview him thoroughly and offer him protection and a new identity under the government's Witness Protection Program. They went to their homes to pack and planned to leave first thing in the morning.

CHAPTER 15

The KGB staff in the embassy in Washington, D.C. had a meeting every day with Kerensky. He was starting to get pressure from Moscow to either locate the young Alex Nicola boy or have Operative Piotr Blok transferred back to Moscow. Kerensky didn't want to lose Blok, one of his best operatives.

Moscow headquarters of the KGB was starting to worry. If the FBI learned Blok and the KGB were responsible for the Nicola murders, it would be a black mark for the Soviets and the "points" lost in diplomatic channels would have a ripple effect right up to the Russian Premier. Locating Alex had become the highest priority of the embassy and the pressure was starting to get to Kerensky.

Every day, Gagari Putin was asked if his finance, Anna Bukhart, found any information coming into the Social Security records in the names of Alex Nicola or James Alan Smith. And every day Gagari always answered that Anna's checks had not found any new information. The same was asked of the embassy operative who handled the informant in the Driver's License Bureau, and the answer was also, "Nothing."

A daily review of the taped calls on the Smith's telephone did not help in locating Alex. Technicians particularly listened when Jimmy Smith was on the line. Several of his friends asked if he'd heard from Alex and he told them he hadn't.

Kerensky was now seeing the two black prostitutes every other day. Maybe it was the pressure of the current situation, maybe it was the herbal recipe he started taking to enhance male performance, he wasn't sure. What he didn't know was the younger of the two prostitutes had been contacted by the FBI and agreed to be an informant for them.

The day Agents Emerson and Brewer left for Beckley, WV, Anna Bukhart spotted a new entry in the Social Security files of withholding in the name of James Alan Smith, Friendship Mining Company, Beckley, WV. She quickly telephoned Gagari at the embassy and within hours, two KGB operatives with high school yearbook photos of Alexander Nicola were headed for Beckley, West Virginia. One was a KGB veteran, Gregor, the other was, Elana, who was in her third and final year of probationary field training.

The two intelligence agencies, with agents dispatched to the small town of Beckley, had no idea the other one knew of Alex's whereabouts. The KGB only had the employment record that a James Alan Smith was working at the Friendship Mining Company. The FBI had an address and vehicle description both in the name of James

Alan Smith. As they drove toward Beckley, both sets of agents discussed the limited information they had. The two Russians were taking the lead more lightly speculating this could be a "wild goose chase," since James Alan Smith was a fairly common name. In any event, the Russians were just happy to get away from Washington and out from under the strict rules and regulations of the embassy.

In truth, both agencies' apprehensions had some basis, since the names: James, Alan and Smith were the most common first, middle and last names in the U.S. When KGB operative Piotr Blok found out about the lead at Beckley he wanted to be part of the team going there. However, he was informed by Major General Kerensky the lead was speculative and he might be more urgently needed at the embassy if new information developed.

Agents Emerson and Brewer arrived at Beckley around 7 p.m. They found rooms at a Motel 6, and after checking in, grabbed two quick sandwiches at a Braums. After eating, they set out to find the address for Jimmy Smith.

CHAPTER 16

Alex decided to take in a movie that same evening. He had plenty of time before clocking in for his midnight to eight shift. The boarding house evening dinner was roast beef with mashed potatoes, gravy and butternut squash. He was never been a big fan of squash, but tonight he thought it wasn't all that bad.

After dinner, he decided to leave the boarding house a little early to do some shopping for a small gift for Mary. Alex and Mary had now dated several times and he had grown very fond of her. He liked her simple outlook on life, strong moral values and admired her strong Christian faith. Their physical relationship had only developed to a "good night kiss." He was ready to go a little farther and start seeing her more often.

He got into the Impala, which he was starting to like even more than Jimmy Smith's Cutlass. He started it up and drove out of the parking lot. Turning right onto the street, he headed to the downtown area just a few blocks away. The sun had set and it was starting to turn dark.

Two minutes away, and not seeing the Impala leave the boarding house parking lot, Agents Emerson and Brewer were slowly driving, trying to read house numbers. When they found the boarding house, they drove around the block and pulled into an alley behind the building. Carefully approaching the cars parked behind the boarding house, the agents were squinting in efforts to find the 1972 Impala. It was not there.

The KGB Agents, Gregor and Elana, having left Washington, D.C. later than their FBI counterparts, decided to stop for the night and head on to Beckley in the morning. They saw a sign on I-64 that read, "Lewisburg 2 Miles," with an arrow pointing south.

The Lewisburg Motel had a small dim light shining over an entrance and a faded neon sign that said, "Office." There were 10-15 rooms all with outside entrances. It appeared to the Russians that about half of the rooms were occupied, based on the cars parked in front of motel room doors. Elana pointed out a convenience and liquor store across the street. They registered as husband and wife using false names with ID's in the false names if needed. The clerk, an older gentleman who looked like it was past his bedtime, didn't stop to check ID's or the false license number Gregor put down on the registration.

After paying cash for the room, the Soviet agents drove across the road to the convenience store. They bought a bottle of cheap vodka and a package of hotdog buns to go with the two cans of Russian stew they brought with them. At the room, Elana quickly opened the vodka and splashed a generous portion into a plastic glass and handed it to her partner. She smiled at him as he took the glass. He gulped a huge swig of the liquor, watching her pour herself a glassful. They both made eye contact and giggled a little.

Two more big swigs by both were now starting to give them warm, sexual feelings. Elana looked down at Gregor's crotch, pointed at the bulge and started laughing. It wasn't long before they started taking their clothes off as they were engaged in deep, tongue probing kisses. They never got around to eating the stew and buns that night.

CHAPTER 17

Alex did find a silver bracelet with a small silver heart for Mary. He would give it to her in the morning upon completion of his shift. After the movie, he headed for the mine company. The FBI parked two houses away in the alley behind the boarding house. They decided to wait for a few hours in hopes of spotting the Impala. At midnight, they gave up and headed back to their motel.

The next morning, the KGB Agents ate the stew and hotdog buns for breakfast. Then they headed out, continuing to the town of Beckley and the Friendship Mining Company. Their instructions were to not blow their cover and take all necessary precautions to not let anyone know someone was looking for James Alan Smith. If it was Alex Nicola, their task was to kill him. The plan was to set up where they could survey the office and employees coming and going at the mining company building.

After asking at a gas station, the Russians were given directions to the mining company. They arrived that morning at 10:45. Alex had clocked out, talked to Mary for a few minutes and had given her the bracelet. They made plans for a dinner date for the weekend and he left the office at 8:30 a.m.

As Alex pulled into the back parking lot of the boarding house, he yawned and turned off the ignition. He grabbed his lunch sack, headed into the building and went upstairs to his apartment. Emerson and Brewer, located in the same spot as the previous evening, watched as the 1972 Impala drove into the lot. They saw the person driving exit the car and walk into the boarding house. Agent Brewer pulled out photos of Alex and glanced at them.

He turned to Emerson and said, "Boy, I don't know, do you think that's him?"

"Well, he's about the right height and build, but it's hard to say. His hair is darker, and then there's the beard and that stocking cap," replied Emerson. They decided to try to get another look at the driver and maybe a photograph before making a call to their supervisor. They got a camera ready, leaned back and started to wait.

Gregor and Elana watched people come and go from the mine office all day long and found themselves dozing off a few times. They never saw anyone who resembled Alex Nicola. By late afternoon and after discussing their love making from the previous night, they decided to call it a day and find a motel for some early sex. Elana suggested they could always pick up sandwiches later at some drive-thru place.

Agents Emerson and Brewer waited most of the morning to spot the driver of the Impala. Finally they decided to take turns walking to find a restroom and getting a sandwich while the other one stayed in the car.

Alex awoke at 2 p.m. and went downstairs to see the landlady. She always made up sandwiches for his lunch and one for him to take to work. Today, she made up not only a sandwich but put together a plate of food from lunch. As he was starting to go back upstairs, she stopped him and told him something came in the mail for him. She retrieved a package from the front hallway and gave it to him. He saw it was from a stamp company in New York City. He had ordered some Russian stamp album pages for new issues a few weeks back. After eating the plate of food, Alex got out some Russian stamps and began mounting them on the new pages.

Since arriving in Beckley, Alex had been cautious about doing anything that could be traced. He didn't open up a checking account and paid everything in cash. The landlady and Lefty didn't seem to mind that he didn't pay them with a check. He ordered stamps on several occasions by looking at ads in stamp publications at the library. He paid for them with postal money orders, as he did with the new Russian album pages.

He was always a little saddened whenever he worked with his Russian stamps because it reminded him of his family. He often wondered how the investigation was going. Thinking of his family, he got up and looked out the window. He didn't see anything unusual and told himself he was being foolish. He had it pretty good here in Beckley. But he never forgot someone might eventually come looking for him and he had to be ready to leave immediately. So far, he had not seen anything or anyone that seemed out of the ordinary or looked suspicious. That was about to change.

CHAPTER 18

The KGB Agents returned to the Friendship Mining Company location about 7:30 that evening and resumed watching employees enter and exit the main building. Before leaving the motel a little earlier, they phoned the embassy and spoke with Boris Kerensky. Gregor lied to him that they split up and were watching the plant day and night. Elana smiled a little when she heard her partner tell this lie to their boss. He told them if they didn't spot Alex Nicola in the next day or so, they should plan on making a pretext call to the mining office. They hoped to learn if he still worked there and if so, the hours he worked.

At approximately 6 p.m., Emerson and Brewer were ready for a break and needed to call their supervisor. They wanted to let him know what they knew at this point. Agent Emerson walked to a gas station, used the restroom and made the call. Then he bought a sandwich, a cup of coffee, and returned to the car. He gave Agent Brewer directions to the gas station and updated him on his conversation with their supervisor. The supervisor was glad to hear from Emerson and advised him nothing new had developed on the boy's location. He told him the Beckley lead was the only thing they had going at the time. After taking their breaks, both men settled back in the car and waited.

Alex got ready to go to work and left the boarding house, allowing himself about 30 minutes to get to the mining office. When he came out of the entrance, the FBI Agents spotted him immediately. They started up their car and as Alex drove his Impala out of the parking lot onto the street, they slowly pulled forward to follow.

Gregor was nodding on and off and Elana was standing outside the car having a cigarette, when young Alex pulled into the mining company lot. She saw him first and tapped on the car window. He sat up and they both took notice. What they observed was a young man about the age of Alex Nicola, but his hair was darker and longer, and he had a beard.

They wrote down the license number and description of the car he was driving. They were so enthralled with the possibility this was indeed, Alex Nicola, they didn't see the four-door, dark colored FBI sedan. Agents Emerson and Brewer had pulled into the lot and were following the Impala to the back parking lot of the plant.

When Alex pulled into the main gate and as he drove through the front parking lot, his headlights flashed on a blonde woman standing next to a car smoking a cigarette. *That's strange. What's she doing out here at this time of night?* She was watching his car and he saw a man inside her car looking his way. Alex proceeded to the back lot.

He stopped the car and turned off the ignition. He sat there for a few minutes and thought about the woman he just saw. He looked back but didn't see their car. Emerson and Brewer exited the FBI car and approached the Impala. As Alex was getting out of his car, the men pulled out their picture ID's and identified themselves as FBI Agents. Emerson asked him if he was Alex Nicola. He only hesitated for a second, and said, "Yes, I'm Alex Nicola."

Emerson, not wanting to attract any attention, quickly said they needed to talk to him and asked Alex when and where they could later meet. He told them he had to go to work in a few minutes and maybe they could meet about 8:30 in the morning at the coffee shop next to Lefty's Used Cars. They agreed and went back to the FBI car.

As he walked into the mine company office, he wondered if he should have mentioned to the FBI that it looked like a woman and man were watching him. That night, he asked his supervisor if he could get off a little early. He wondered if the man and woman he'd seen would still be around.

The Soviet agents called it quits when they saw the young man enter the building obviously starting his shift, and assumed it was probably midnight to 8 a.m. They would return in the morning and follow him when he left the parking lot. They still weren't positive the person they saw was Alex Nicola.

Emerson and Brewer were at the small coffee shop by 8:15 the next morning. It had three booths, a counter with five stools and four tables. There were about 7-9 people in the shop when they walked in. Of course, everyone looked at them as they took a booth. They were wearing Dickies work shirts and pants. Brewer was wearing an older, somewhat sweat stained ball cap. If anyone asked, they were just passing through Beckley headed for Texas to work in the oil fields.

Gregor and Elana were in place at 7:30 that morning planning to take some photos and follow the Impala when the driver left the mining company parking lot. They had no idea Alex left about 30 minutes before they arrived.

CHAPTER 19

Alex walked into the coffee shop 30 minutes later and joined the two FBI Agents in a booth.

"Good morning," said Agent Emerson.

He responded, "Morning," as he looked around the room.

"So, you been here before?" asked Emerson.

"Couple of times," answered Alex. He noticed the other agent studying the menu when the waitress walked up and handed him a menu. Both men were drinking black coffee.

"Coffee, honey?" she asked in a monotone voice, probably using her usual greeting.

"Yes, with cream and sugar." She turned and walked away.

Emerson leaned over and in a low voice told Alex they thought he was in grave danger. He added that the FBI could offer him a new identity under the Department of Justice's Witness Protection Program. Emerson looked around the room and then continued, "We can relocate you where no one would know you and pay you enough to cover most of your expenses."

The waitress returned with Alex's cup of coffee and a pot. She sat the cup in front of him and refilled the agent's cups, maneuvering the cup and the pot in an obvious, well-practiced routine.

"You boys ready to order?" They all nodded and ordered quickly from a menu featuring several breakfast specials. She thanked them in passing, grabbed the menus and headed for the kitchen.

Alex leaned forward and thinking about the woman with

the cigarette, quietly asked, "Who's looking for me and why am I in grave danger?"

Emerson took the question and answered, "Your father was involved with the KGB and we believe they are responsible for murdering your family. We think you can identify the Russian contact your father was seeing and believe they think so, too." Alex started to mention the two people he saw in the mining company parking lot, but decided not to.

Alex looked down and added some cream and sugar to his coffee. "I don't know about all this. Let me think about it and give you my decision tomorrow." The agents nodded in agreement and they all three sat in silence for a few minutes. Finally the food started arriving and the girl refilled their cups. They ate without speaking and when they finished, Emerson suggested they meet again the next day but somewhere other than the cafe. Alex suggested the library, just down the street a few blocks and they agreed to meet at 10 a.m.

The Russians were getting worried. It was past 8 a.m.

and they hadn't spotted the Impala or the driver they saw the night before. They finally decided the driver must have gotten the day off or called in sick. They discussed going back to the motel for more screwing, but decided against it when they remembered the maid had to clean the room. So, they opted to head downtown and get some breakfast.

The FBI Agents left ahead of Alex, who had to use the restroom. After visiting the restroom and as he approached the front door of the cafe, it opened and he heard a man say something in Russian. He was holding the door open for a woman and looking at her, and not in Alex's direction. He recognized the pair as the man and woman he saw watching him the night before. They both stepped to one side and each reached to hold the door open for Alex. When they did, he noticed they were in very casual, tourist-like clothes. He looked down as he passed them going out the door.

Gregor and Elana looked at each other. They knew they couldn't just start to follow him, so they entered the cafe. Thinking quickly, Gregor motioned for the waitress and getting her attention, asked what time they opened in the morning. She said, "6 a.m. honey." He thanked her and they exited the coffee shop. As luck would have it, they turned left out the door and walked quickly in efforts to spot Alex, who had turned right after exiting the coffee shop. "That was him," blurted out Elana as they started walking.

"I know," said Gregor.

After seeing the man and woman at the coffee shop's door, Alex ducked behind Lefty's office and hid behind a dumpster. After an hour or so, he sneaked down the alley away from the boarding house and within a couple of blocks, circled back. He kept looking in every direction as he walked, headed toward the boarding house.

He didn't see the man and woman's car anywhere and it was not in the boarding house lot. He quickly entered the residence and proceeded to his apartment. There he carefully spent the next 30 to 40 minutes peeking through the curtains. He didn't see the man and the woman or their car. Finally, Alex lay down on the bed and started assessing his situation.

CHAPTER 20

The Russians never did see Alex after they left the coffee shop. They stayed together to appear to be a couple and not cause any undue suspicion. After walking hurriedly away from the shop for several blocks and looking both ways as they came to cross streets, they decided he must have gone the other direction. They went one block east and then headed back north, or the opposite direction they were taking….still no sign of him. After a half hour or so, they gave up and headed back to their car.

They had several things going for them. They knew it was Alex, where he worked, his hours and what car he was driving. They drove back out to the Friendship Mining Company and drove slowly through the parking lot. His car was not there. From there they decided to drive around town, looking for the Impala. While doing so, they both discussed what story they were going to relay to Major General Boris Kerensky about what they had accomplished. They decided to tell him they had spotted Alex and his car but were stopped by a train crossing and lost him.

If they said they had actual physical contact with him and didn't kill him, it might piss off the Major General and add demerits to their annual performance ratings. If they told him they hadn't spotted him, he may order them back to Washington, and they didn't want that, just yet. They were enjoying the sex too much.

Gregor stopped at a pay phone on the side of a gas station and reported the train story to Kerensky. He seemed encouraged and told them to split up, each working 12 hour shifts so they could be looking for him around the clock. He told them the Smith's phone tap had still not developed any information of value.

When Gregor got back in the car he looked at Elana and said with a slight smirk on his face, "He said, good job, go have sex," and she busted out laughing. They drove to a liquor store, were elated to find the store had Stolichnaya Russian Vodka and headed back to their motel.

Now, also back at the motel, Special Agent Emerson made a call to his supervisor. He told him they located Alex and discussed his danger and the option of him going into the Witness Protection Program. The supervisor asked if they had seen any KGB Agents and Emerson told him they hadn't. Emerson said they were to meet with Alex again in the morning. The supervisor told Emerson to give him another day or so to decide. It was a big decision, especially for an eighteen year old.

CHAPTER 21

In his boarding house room, Alex got up from the bed and retrieved a plastic bag taped to the headboard. He opened the bag and counted the bills. There were 550 dollars. He lay back down. The FBI might be able to protect him right away and maybe he would tell them in the morning about the unknown man and woman. *Could they be KGB Agents?*

He got up again and looked carefully out the window. Still didn't see them or their car. He lay back down. He thought about what the FBI said about the Witness Protection Plan. *How soon would that happen? And what about in the meantime?* In a funny sort of way, it did kind of appeal to him. Alex slowly drifted into a deep sleep.

He dreamed he was being chased by a large black shadow. He was running through the streets of his old neighborhood and the shadow was slowly catching up with him. His legs were getting so tired that he finally fell and looking up saw the shadow was actually a man with a mask over his eyes and he was holding a gun pointed at him. Alex woke himself up with his own half groan and half scream. He looked around and it took him a minute to get his bearings and realize he was in his boarding house room.

A wonderful aroma was in the air. The landlady must be cooking supper and he checked his clock radio. It was almost 5 p.m. He lay on the bed a little longer. His options were limited but the fear of the strange man and the woman, who were probably KGB, helped him decide. The fastest and safest thing to do is what he did when he found out about his family being murdered, flee.

The boarding house supper was usually right at 6 o'clock and Alex was there a few minutes before. He had his bags packed and would have to leave a few of his things. He planned to leave Beckley, WV right after he finished eating. He wouldn't say anything to anyone and pretend it was just another normal day and a normal meal.

Near the end of the meal, one of the residents, a talkative sort who liked to argue about the pros and cons of various professional baseball teams tried to engage Alex in expressing his views. Alex told him he really didn't follow baseball all that much. That set the guy off and he went on and on about how people don't appreciate the great game of baseball anymore. Alex quickly finished his dessert of apple pie, wiped his mouth with the napkin and excused himself, saying he had to get ready for a date.

A half hour later, using the back stairs of the boarding house, Alex carried his things to the car, got in and headed south on the interstate that runs through Beckley. He had no idea where he was going, but only that he felt good about getting out of town. He knew he could always contact the FBI later, if he decided to take them up on their offer. His heart was heavy, however, knowing he'd probably never see Mary again. He started to choke up a little and it took him a few minutes to regain his composure. He thought maybe, just maybe he'd be able to return to Beckley, some day.

CHAPTER 22

Anton Pavlovich, KGB Commander in Moscow, was getting briefed daily by Kerensky from the secure telephone at the Russian Embassy. He only made his calls directly to Pavlovich late at night at his home in Moscow or at his dacha. He knew the concerns and questions would be fewer and less pointed by Pavlovich if he had partaken of his favorite vodka before the call. It was also much easier to enhance the truth of the matter, putting an unsuccessful effort to find young Alex in a better light.

Pavlovich would not remember all the details the next day, even with a clear head. Kerensky knew him too well.

However, in this night's late call to the Commander's Moscow home, he was able to at least report some progress. In this report he added even more bullshit to make it sound like he was pulling out all stops and the whole embassy was working around the clock, which was pure poppycock. The progress he planned to report to Pavlovich was the information he got earlier from Agent Gregor about the boy being spotted but got away when they had to stop for a train in Beckley.

As he was relaying the events of the day at Beckley and the near miss of killing Alex, Boris heard a cork pop and a splashing noise coming from Pavlovich's end. Boris smiled to himself, knowing a little more vodka would make his report even more believable.

He went on and on how his men nearly had Alex in their grasps several times that day, but there was always someone with him so they were not able to finish him off. He added some more heroic efforts before finishing with how he got away when the agents had to stop for train track safety arms coming down at a street crossing. Kerensky heard Pavlovich mumble something about the damn Americans and their train crossings. Before hanging up, he assured the Commander, they would find Alex tomorrow and kill him.

After hanging up, Boris knew he had bought at least another day or two and dialed his secretary Yakov. Waking up Yakov was not a concern of the embassy's Major General, he had other things on his mind. "A black, and a blonde white woman?" he echoed his boss's request.

"That's right and for 10 o'clock in the morning," added Kerensky.

Yakov looked at the clock beside his bed. It was the middle of the night and he'd have only a couple of hours in the morning to try to line up the girls per the Major General's order. "Yes, sir," he responded, and he heard the phone click on the other end. Kerensky got up and retrieved a bottle of vodka. Now it was his turn to relax a little, then get some sleep so he could fully enjoy the two women in the morning.

CHAPTER 23

Alex drove the speed limit. He wanted to get out of West Virginia as fast as he could but didn't want to get stopped or draw any attention. He stopped at rest areas to use the restroom and to buy black coffee and candy bars. This kept him awake and he didn't have to stop at cafés for food. When he needed gas, he picked a pump as far from the office as possible. He also made sure his knit hat was pulled down low and he minimized any conversations with station attendants.

The sign said, "Tuscaloosa 20 Miles." He glanced down

at his gas gauge. It was nearing empty. He looked at his watch, it was almost 5 a.m. and he was hungry. He pulled off the interstate onto Highway 82, to Tuscaloosa. Arriving in town, he spotted a Waffle House on his right and next to it was a Sinclair Gas Station.

At the gas station he bought a small Rand-McNally Road Atlas and after looking at his options, decided to stay on Highway 82, heading west. After gassing up, he drove to the Waffle House. He ordered, "The He-Man's Special," of three eggs, three strips of bacon, hash browns, waffle and coffee.

As he drove west on 82, Alex thought about where he was going and decided he would have to stop before too long and get some rest. He saw on the map that 82 would take him all the way into Texas and maybe he would stop there and start looking for a job in the oil fields. He drove on till he got to Columbus, Mississippi, where he spotted a Wal-Mart as he entered the city limits.

He pulled into the lot and parked on the side of the building where it looked like the employees parked. He went inside to use the restroom. A doughnut display sat just inside the entry. Alex decided to buy a small package of powdered donuts, which he planned to eat after he got some sleep. Back in the car, he pulled the lever to move the driver's seat back. He closed his eyes and within a few minutes fell into a deep sleep.

Agents Emerson and Brewer waited at the library for over an hour. They finally decided to drive by the boarding house and look for Alex's car. It was not there. They drove around Beckley for several more hours looking for the car but didn't see it. Emerson telephoned his supervisor. He instructed Emerson and his partner to contact Alex's landlady and make appropriate inquiries.

The two KGB Agents, Gregor and Elana, had an exhausting night of sex and consuming two bottles of vodka. They slept in till 11a.m. With pounding headaches they forced themselves to find a place to eat and then planned to drive by the coffee shop. They didn't see Alex's car anywhere in town.

They drove around town for a couple more hours.

While doing so, they discussed their next call to Kerensky. They couldn't put it off much longer and had no idea what they were going to tell him. At 2 p.m. they decided to make the call. They were told he was out and to call back in a couple of hours.

Gregor and Elana looked at each other, smiled and headed back to the motel room. At the room they hung the, "Do Not Disturb," sign on the outside door knob, stripped off their clothes and jumped into bed. At the same time, Boris Kerensky was being entertained by the black woman and the white blonde. Their romping all recorded on one of the FBI's miniature cameras, secretly hidden in a decorative bedroom wall hanging.

Emerson and Brewer found the landlady busy cleaning up in the kitchen of the boarding house. They identified themselves and said they needed to talk to Jimmy Smith on a routine matter. She told them Jimmy was probably asleep in his room because he worked nights and slept during the day. She showed them to his upstairs room and she stood back as Emerson knocked on the door.

There was no answer. He knocked again, this time a little louder and there was still no answer. After a few minutes, the agents asked the landlady to open the door with her master key. When she did and they entered the room, it was obvious to all of them that Alex Nicola, aka, Jimmy Smith had taken off with most of his personal belongings. When they made their report to the supervisor, he told them to return to Washington.

After a couple of hours of on again, off again sex, the two Soviet agents decided to retry a call to reach Kerensky. This time he was back at the embassy and with his ashes newly hauled, had a clearer, well-focused mind. Upon hearing they couldn't find Alex, he very pointedly instructed them to spend the rest of the day looking for the car. If they didn't find it, they were to go to the mining company office before closing and using some pretext try to find out if Alex was still around.

The two Russians were delighted to have another day in Beckley. Both knew they were supposed to be working hard to find Alex, but in actuality were more interested in each other. Gregor and Elana had reached the point where they couldn't care less whether they ever found Alex again.

CHAPTER 24

Alex woke from hearing a horn honk some distance away. He looked at his watch. It was nearly 7 p.m. and getting dark. He sat up and decided to eat his donuts. When he was done he saw a McDonald's sign a little further down the road and headed that way. After a restroom stop, he bought a large black coffee and got back on Highway 82, continuing west.

After several hours he had to use a restroom. He was approaching Greenville, Mississippi and a quick glance at his map showed a rest area between Greenville and the

Arkansas border. It was nearing 11 p.m. when he pulled into the rest area. A car was backing out of one of the diagonal parking spots and one other car was parked a few spots away from that one. Alex pulled into the spot that was just vacated and picking up his trash in the car, got out and headed for the rest area building. He noticed there were no outside lights in the front of the building, only a dim light coming from inside. After tossing his trash into a bin, he entered the building and went to the men's room.

When he came out of the men's room, it occurred to him there was hardly a sound inside the building and as he opened the door to exit, saw the same car he saw before still parked a few spots from his. He took one step and heard a rustling noise behind and to one side of him. As Alex started to turn to look he felt a hard whack to his head and suddenly the world started spinning.

The next thing he knew he heard a muffled voice. Someone was saying something, but he didn't understand what they were saying. He was lying on the concrete in front of the rest area entrance. His head was pounding and he had the worst headache he'd ever had. He looked up and saw an older couple bent over with a look of concern in their eyes.

"Are you okay?" one of them asked. He lifted his arm and felt the area of his head where it hurt the worst. He looked at his fingers and saw they were covered with blood. The older gentleman started dabbing Alex's head with his handkerchief. The woman repeated, "Are you okay?"

It was at that moment Alex realized he'd been robbed. He looked in the direction of the car he saw earlier. It was gone. He fumbled for his billfold. It was empty. *They took all my money.* He looked at the couple and realizing his dilemma, started to cry. He saw blood on his hands and his head felt like his skull was crushed.

He heard the woman saying, "There, there now. It'll be all right."

The man said, "Shall we call the police?"

Alex said, "No, I didn't see anyone or could give them a description of a car. I'll be okay."

Putting his arms around Alex, the man said, "Let me help you sit up."

The woman asked, "What happened?" Alex was still sobbing and pulled his handkerchief from his pocket. He wiped his eyes, took a deep breath and stopped sobbing. The man and the woman were still hovering over him with concerned looks.

Alex said, "Someone must have hit me over the head when I was coming out of the building. They took all my money."

"Oh, dear," exclaimed the woman and the man looked up to scan the parking area.

The talking and breathing seemed to somewhat help the pain, but it was still pretty bad. He looked up at the man and said, "Can you please help me up?" The man put his hand under one of Alex's arms and started lifting. He felt better standing up and looked at the couple one at a time.

"Did you see anyone leaving, or a car or anything?" he asked the couple.

"Why no, we didn't. There was only the one car in

front when we pulled into the parking area."

Alex looked toward the parking area. He saw his car. "Yeah, that's my car."

The gentleman motioned toward the drinking fountain and Alex took a few hesitant steps in that direction. He drank as much as he could and the bending over to drink caused his head to start pounding even more than before. The woman pulled something out of her purse. "Here, take a couple of these aspirins," and handed them to Alex. He took them, drank some more water and thanked them for stopping to help him.

He pulled out his wallet again, as if he couldn't believe his money was gone. The wallet was empty, but they left his driver's license, the last payment stub from Lefty's Used Cars and his last payment stub from the Friendship Mining Company. "You want us to take you to the hospital?" asked the man.

Alex looked at him and shook his head. "No, I'm starting to feel a little better already. I'll be okay, I guess."

The woman motioned something to her husband. The

man took out a money clip and handed Alex a 20 dollar bill. “Here son, take this. It’s not much but it will get you to the next town, at least.” He took the money without even thinking about it and again thanked the couple. They entered the rest area building and Alex went to his car.

CHAPTER 25

When he got in, he saw money in the storage consul. He forgot he still had change from a twenty he used to buy the coffee at McDonalds. With the twenty the older couple gave him he had about 39 dollars. He started the Impala and looked at the gas gauge. It showed a little over half full. He backed out of the parking spot and waved at the couple who were now coming out of the building. He didn't know what he was going to do, but pulled back onto Highway 82 and headed the car west.

Alex knew he would have to stop somewhere and get a

job before he ran out of money. Maybe stay just long enough to be able to afford to continue through Texas and possibly try to get into Mexico. His head was feeling much better, maybe it was the aspirin. To his surprise, he didn't feel tired and so he kept heading west.

When he got to Texarkana, Arkansas the sun was just starting to show itself in his rear view mirror. He needed to find a restroom and was getting a little hungry. He looked at his gas gauge and saw he was about out of gas. Alex saw a truck stop ahead and pulled in.

He bought $10 in gas, a bagel and a cup of coffee. He put a lot of cream and sugar in the coffee. He now had only $26.50. Across the street from the truck stop was a hospital. Alex decided to park in the hospital lot. After he finished his bagel and coffee, he'd try to get some sleep.

The two Russian agents spent one more day driving around Beckley. Just before the mining office closed, Gregor went inside and approached the girl at the reception desk. He gave her a false name and told her he met Jimmy Smith at the local coffee shop the day before.

He said Jimmy told him he worked for the mining company and they were supposed to have breakfast together again in the morning. However, something had come up and the man told the girl he was not going to be able to meet Jimmy in the morning but didn't know how to contact him. He asked the girl, who was Mary, for Jimmy's phone number and address.

Mary told Gregor she couldn't give out employee information but Jimmy did not show up for work the night before. They didn't know if he was sick or not, or if he would come to work for his shift later that evening. She said she would leave a message for him and if he came in to work, she'd make sure he got the man's message he couldn't meet Jimmy at the coffee shop.

Gregor was not satisfied in failing to get Jimmy's address, but decided to leave well enough alone. He thanked the girl and left the mining company office. Back in the car, he told Elana what happened and they decided to tell Kerensky Alex Nicola left Beckley and no one knew where he was headed.

After telling the Major General that Nicola had left Beckley, he ordered them to return to Washington the next day. The Russians had one more night together. They celebrated their last night together by buying two bottles of Stolichnaya, but never got around to having sex. They had good intentions but both started hitting the vodka heavily when they got to their room. They never got beyond the kissing and clothes removal stages, before they passed out.

Kerensky had to report to Moscow he had again failed to find the young Nicola boy. He waited to call Commander Pavlovich till it was near midnight in Russia. He again hoped to catch him at least half way through another bottle of vodka. The Commander was slightly slurring his responses when he told him Nicola had slipped away and was no longer in Beckley. Kerensky smiled as he talked and knew he'd be able to easily convince the KGB head that they had sources hard at work and would be back on young Alex Nicola's trail within days, if not sooner. Pavlovich bought it, hook, line and sinker.

The FBI didn't put out an APB to law enforcement on

Alex's 1972 Chevrolet Impala, since they didn't have an arrest warrant. They decided to again contact Department of Motor Vehicle departments in each state, posting a, "Stop," to merely notify the nearest office of the FBI on any new registrations for the car. By law they could not have access to the records and files of the Social Security Administration unless it was a case of treason or to locate a military AWOL. However, that did not preclude having sources within that government agency who could be asked to review certain files. That source started checking every day for any new employment earnings that may have come in for a James Alan Smith.

CHAPTER 26

Alex woke up and the sun was shining brightly. He felt very refreshed and while sitting there, he saw someone come around the corner of the hospital and approach his car. For some strange reason the guy reminded him of Jimmy. Something about the way he walked, maybe? He thought about Jimmy and wondered how he was doing. He thought about giving him a call and apologizing about taking his wallet and car. *Or maybe a letter?* He decided to call and went back to the convenience store across from the hospital and bought a prepaid calling card. It was good for ten minutes of long distance. It cost him $2.75. He used the store's pay phone booth located next to the sidewalk running in front of the store.

He called the Smith's. Mrs. Smith answered and when Alex asked if Jimmy was home, she said, "Just a minute," and he heard her holler, "Jimmy, it's for you." There were a few moments of silence then he heard, "Hello."

He hesitated and then said, "Jimmy, its Alex."

"Alex, where are you?"

"I'm, a, a, in Texas. Man, I'm sorry about taking your billfold and car, I, I, ah, just didn't know what else to do."

Jimmy sighed and asked, "Are you okay?"

"Yeah, I'm okay."

"What are you going to do?"

"I got to find a job. I'm almost out of money."

Jimmy quickly declared, "Hey I could wire you some money. I could send it to a Western Union nearest to you."

"Look I can't talk too long. I just wanted to apologize for what I did. I hope we're still friends," Alex murmured.

"Alex, it's all right, I'm just glad you're okay. Look, I've got a100 bucks I saved from my birthday money, I could wire it to you this afternoon or first thing in the morning."

"Thanks, man. That would be great. I'm in Texarkana, ah, Texarkana, Texas."

"Okay," said Jimmy. "I'll get the money wired as soon as I can. Okay?"

"Thanks, I better go, oh and Jimmy?"

"Yeah."

"Send it to Jimmy Smith."

"Oh, right, okay," said Jimmy as he heard Alex hang up.

The FBI technical support employee, who was monitoring Smith's telephone, immediately buzzed the supervisor in charge of locating Alex Nicola. Details of the call were relayed from the supervisor to Agents Emerson and Brewer. Several FBI light aircraft were hangered and flew out of a small commercial airport located on the outskirts of Washington, D.C. Pilot agents rotated shifts on a "standby" basis. A call to the agent on duty that day was made and he was told to be ready to fly Agents Emerson and Brewer to Texarkana within a couple of hours. As soon as they arrived at that airport, the agent pilot had a Cessna 182RGS ready to go and they left within minutes.

In the meantime, the supervisor called the FBI's Resident Agency at Texarkana and spoke with the Senior Resident Agent. They were to meet Agents Emerson and Brewer at the Texarkana airport, assist them and provide as much backup as necessary to assure everyone's safety.

It was a couple of hours later that the KGB caught the conversation between Alex and Jimmy. Kerensky ordered two of his agents to charter a flight to Texarkana and get to the Western Union location there as soon as possible. This time he sent two male agents, having heard some talk around the embassy that Gregor was overheard bragging he and Elena spent most of their time in Beckley screwing.

Upon hearing the rumors about the couple and their sexual trysts, the Embassy Chief decided to take steps to cozy up to Elana in the near future. Her derrière had not gone unnoticed to him, but knowing she was married to a professional Russian wrestler, he never considered making any advances. That was, up till now. Now the situation had taken on a whole new light, brightened by this new information and Kerensky's insatiable appetite for sexual gratification. As he sat at his desk, he was starting to get aroused. He discreetly reached down and repositioned his semi-erection to a more comfortable position. He buzzed his secretary Yakov and told him to have Elana come to his office. A few minutes later he knocked on his boss's office door and informed him Elana had stepped out of the office for a few hours.

CHAPTER 27

After hanging up from his conversation with Jimmy Smith, Alex checked the phone book for the location of Western Union. When he found the listing, he saw there were two locations, one on the Texas side of town and one on the Arkansas side. He decided to drive by both sites and had no trouble locating both of them. Both places had signs in their windows showing they were open from 10 a.m. to 10 p.m. He decided he would check with each of them later before they closed, and headed for the library he saw while looking for one of the Western Unions.

There was much optimism and an almost bragging air to Kerensky's call to Anton Pavlovich that day. This time, he didn't have to wait till evening to catch his boss half drunk. After passing on the details of the phone call between Alex and his good friend, Jimmy Smith, he assured Pavlovich young Alex would be dead within 24 hours. After hanging up, he took a quick tour of the embassy offices looking for Elana. One of the agents told him she wasn't feeling well and went home. He returned to his desk, somewhat disappointed but anxious to discuss a special assignment he had in mind for her. An "assignment," she would be obligated to accept.

Alex read through several of the national newspapers and not seeing anything that caught his interest decided to head back to one of the Western Union offices. He was closest to the one just off the main highway in downtown Texarkana, Texas, so he proceeded to that location.

As Alex was walking out of the library, Agents Emerson and Brewer were getting off the plane and were greeted by four of the Texarkana agents. They formed two teams for surveillance of both Western Union locations. One headed by Agent Emerson, the other by Agent Brewer. Each briefed the other agents as they started driving to their assigned locations. Emerson and Brewer gave each agent a copy of the latest description of Alex and the car he was driving.

Alex was surprised they had already received the wire from Jimmy Smith. It had been just a little over three hours since he spoke to Jimmy. He presented his driver's license and the clerk looked at him, a little in disbelief when he saw the wire came from a, "Jimmy Smith," to a, "James Alan Smith." Alex just assumed a nonchalant demeanor, like he was doing business as usual and kept looking at the guy. The clerk proceeded to count out $100 in ten dollar bills. There was a small charge for the service, which Jimmy paid for when he sent the money.

The two KGB operatives rented a car when they arrived at the airport at Texarkana, Texas. Using fake ID's they told the clerk they would need the car for a few days. When asked by the nosy young clerk why they were in town and could he give them any directions, they told him they represented a foreign company looking for a location to build a motel. When he asked the name of the motel, one of the agents muttered, "You've never heard of it," and they walked away with the clerk staring at them.

Alex exited the Western Union office and walked to his car. He was trying to decide if he should spend the night somewhere in the area or get back on the road. If he stayed, it would cost for a motel. If he continued on down the road he would save motel money, but eventually would have to find a place to get some rest.

The Russians were given only one address in Texarkana for Western Union. The embassy analyst made the false assumption there would only be one office in Texarkana and the city was only in Arkansas. The address for Western Union on the Arkansas side was where they headed.

The FBI teams arrived at both Western Union locations at about the same time and each confirmed they were in place by radio communication. Agent Emerson spotted the 1972 Impala parked on the south side of the building with the Western Union office. He directed the agent driving to go around the block to get in a better position to watch the Impala.

Just before Alex got to his car, he stopped to put the $100 cash into his billfold. Suddenly he heard a noise outside the Western Union's front door. Someone was yelling in Spanish, swearing and calling someone names. Curious, he walked back around the building to see what was happening. Three Hispanic males were wrestling with a younger Hispanic male on the sidewalk in front of the building. He saw three or four other males standing around hollering and encouraging the fight.

The younger male on the ground was finally able to get to his feet and one of the guys ran at him and knocked him down into the street. Just as that happened, the FBI car was passing the front of the building and had to make a quick stop to avoid running over the fighters. Agent Willie Emerson got out of the car and when he did, he and Alex recognized each other. He saw Alex take off running. Emerson and the other agents, now out of their car, started grabbing the fighters and pulling them off each other.

Alex was shocked to see the FBI Agent who talked to him in Beckley. He made up his mind to get back on the highway as soon as he could. He glanced back at the fight scene. The people involved were walking away and getting into separate vehicles. The agents were scurrying back to their car. Instead of taking either of the main streets away from the building, he drove down an alley, turned onto a street, went one more block and turned down another alley. He did this several more times until he hit a busy four-lane street.

CHAPTER 28

Emerson told the other agents to get back into the car. They resumed their search for Alex's car by circling the Western Union Building. Not spotting the Impala, they all got out of their car and looked all around the building. They still didn't see Alex or the Impala. They drove around the block several more times and finally Agent Emerson said, "It's no use spending any more time here. Looks like breaking up the fight allowed him to slip away."

After several hours waiting at the Western Union location on the Arkansas side of town, the two KGB

Agents decided to go inside posing as a contact for Jimmy Smith. The clerk had no information about any transfer for a Jimmy Smith but did tell them there was another office on the Texas side of town. They proceeded to that location only to find out Jimmy Smith had already been in a couple of hours earlier. They contacted Major General Kerensky at the embassy. He told them to check all the motel and hotel lots for the 1972 Impala. If they spotted Nicola, they were to shoot him on the spot, witnesses or no witnesses.

Within a few miles, the four-lane street Alex was on connected with Interstate 30 West. He wasn't comfortable on a major highway like 30 in case the FBI might be following him. He was also worried that if the FBI could find him, the KGB wouldn't be far behind. At Mt. Pleasant, Texas he got off of 30 and turned south on US Highway 271. After about a half hour, he saw a sign for a road headed west and he took it. He continued to hit roads going south or west till he saw a sign ahead that read, "Lake City, 22 miles."

When he reached the outskirts of the town of Lake

City, he saw a sign, "Lake City, Population 1,988." Alex was getting very tired and he was hungry. He also needed gas and as he entered the downtown area saw a Shell station. He pulled up to one of the pumps and went inside. He gave the clerk $10 for gas, returned to his car and put that amount into his tank. He reentered the station looking for something to eat. Alex saw one aluminum foil wrapped submarine sandwich in one of the glass cases. Apparently it was the last one of who knows how many or how old it was. He didn't care, he was hungry.

He went to the soda cooler and selected a Dr. Pepper. Outside he ate the sandwich and drank half of the soda. He saw an auto repair business across the street and toward the end of the block. There were several cars parked next to and behind the shop. Alex drove over to the lot, noticing a sign, "Harley's Auto Repair." He pulled up next to one of the cars furthest from an outside roof light and went to sleep.

The FBI and the KGB spent the next two days driving around Texarkana looking for Alex and his 1972 Chevrolet

Impala. They both finally gave up and flew back to Washington, D.C. Boris Kerensky was not at all happy with the results both at Beckley and now Texarkana. He would have to make up an even more believable story to relay to KGB Commander Anton Pavlovich.

He decided to tell his Moscow boss his agents shot and injured Alex Nicola in Texarkana, only to be interrupted by a passing police car so they were not able to finish the job. He told a tale of how the agents quickly drove down the wrong way on a one-way street and eluded the police. They were now searching area hospitals and motels looking for Alex and his car. Pavlovich grunted a tacit approval and hung up.

After completing his call to Moscow, Kerensky summoned Elana to his office. He told her he knew how she and Agent Gregor spent most of their time in Beckley. He also told her he wanted her to handle a, "special assignment." She was instructed to meet him at his apartment that evening at 8 p.m.

CHAPTER 29

"Bam, bam, bam," was the sound that woke Alex up. He looked up into the peering eyes of an older, bearded gentleman with a flat top and wearing greasy coveralls. He had a frown on his face and blurted out, "Hey, what do you think this is a motel?"

Finally getting his bearings, Alex rolled down his window. In a stern tone, the old codger continued, "This ain't no motel or motel parking lot. What do you think you're doing, anyway?"

Alex, a little shaken by being woken up from a sound

sleep, finally answered, "I was just getting a little sleep. I meant no harm. I, ah, ah, am just passing through and needed some rest."

The old man stood up, kept staring at Alex and finally said, "Well I guess there's no harm done. If you want I've got some coffee brewing inside and you probably need to use a restroom." Alex nodded an approval. Coffee sounded good to him and he did, indeed, need to use a restroom.

Inside the shop, Harley pointed out the restroom door and he poured out two cups of coffee. When Alex came out of the restroom, Harley asked, "Cream and sugar?"

He uttered a low-toned, "Yes, please," and Harley poured generous amounts of both into Alex's cup.

Harley reached out his hand and said, "I'm Harley Andrews. This is my place. Not much, but it keeps me busy. Where you headed, boy? I see you're from West Virginia, what brings you to Texas?"

He shook Harley's hand and said he was Jimmy Smith and came to Texas to work in the oil fields. Harley was a little taken by Alex's quiet demeanor and he knew the boy was not a threat and wondered if he may be running away from home.

"You got problems back home?" queried Harley.

"Oh, a, ah, no, nothing like that," stammered Alex. "I just thought I'd come out here and make some money for college." He looked out the window and said, "Lake City looks like a nice little town."

"It is," answered Harley. "Been here all my life and it's a nice friendly place to live." He poured Alex some more coffee and began to tell him about the town.

"Lake City was originally settled in 1845 and was a stagecoach stop for the route from Dodge City to Ft. Worth. In the 50's the Corps of Engineers built a dam on the San Joaquin River that ran along the outskirts of town and formed our lake, Lake Sherwood. You like to fish, boy?"

"Ah, a, a, no, I've never been fishing."

While they drank their coffee, Harley went on telling Alex a little about the town. He told him about some of the businesses, including the fairly new Dollar General Store. There were three gas stations, three bars, three churches, a Dairy Queen, a lumber and hardware store, two junk yards, two auto repair shops, a bakery, elevator, motel, library and grocery store. Harley ended his oral tour of the city by adding, "We also got two, oh no, there's three café's, an elevator and a very fine school."

Harley looked at his watch. "I tell you what, boy. It's still early and I haven't had my breakfast yet, what say we go get something to eat."

CHAPTER 30

The mention of something to eat and Alex's growling stomach elicited a, "Well, yeah, a, that sounds good. I'm not in any big hurry to get back on the road." So they walked a couple of blocks to Harley's favorite breakfast spot. Harley ordered his usual sausage and eggs with pancakes and Alex ordered bacon and eggs with hash browns. They chatted over breakfast and coffee but Alex wasn't saying much. Harley sensed the boy didn't want to talk about his home or family, so Harley did most of the talking. He told the boy about his family history and

Scottish heritage. Alex did ask him if he was married and Harley told him his wife died several years ago.

Flashes of his own mother and family suddenly hit him. He swallowed, and holding back some tears, Alex finally said, “I’m sorry to hear that.”

Harley smiled at Alex said, “Oh, it’s okay; we had a lot of good years together.”

While Harley was doing most of the talking, Alex thought he better come up with some kind of a story about his family and where he came from. He decided to tell Harley he was raised in an orphanage in the Washington, D.C. area where he had been abandoned a few days after he was born. And that’s exactly what he did. He told Harley his mother was a young Russian girl who was brought to the US to be a house servant for one of Maryland’s Senators.

“She ran away shortly after I was born and no one ever heard from her again.” He went on saying the orphanage petitioned the State for a birth certificate and gave him the name, “James Alan Smith.”

"When I reached the age of 18, I was free to leave the orphanage, so I did." He said he worked as a dish washer in Washington for a few months. His plan was to save up enough money to come to Texas and find work in the oil fields.

Harley, shaking his head back and forth, said, "Well, that's quite a story, young man." The waitress walked over and laid the check on their table. Harley picked up the check and said, "I've got it."

Alex didn't object and just uttered a quiet, "Thank you."

Back at the repair shop, Alex had to get rid of some of the coffee and when he exited the men's room, Harley commented, "You know if you're not in any hurry to get on down the road, I could use some temporary help around here. Those cars in the back all have to be washed, scrubbed down and waxed because they got sprayed by the railroad a few weeks ago. They were spraying for weeds, the wind came up and some of the elevator's employee's cars got sprayed. The railroad is paying for the clean-up but I've got my hands full for the next few weeks just with car repairs. What dah ya say?"

Alex liked the old man and his friendliness but wasn't sure about the offer. He told Harley he had no place to stay and didn't have much money for a hotel or for food. Harley replied, "Hell son, you could sleep right there," pointing at a sofa sitting along one wall of the office. Alex looked at the sofa. Harley said, "I could advance you a little on your pay to get you by till the end of the week." He was looking at Alex and could tell he was thinking about it.

"The men's room's right there and it's got a shower, towels and everything. That old TV over there isn't used much but it works fine. It might take only a few weeks to do all the cars and I could really use the help."

Alex looked up at Harley and seeing the concern on his face, said, "Yeah, well, maybe I could. I guess it'd be okay."

"Good," replied Harley, "then it's a deal. Let me show you the shop and what has to be done with those cars."

CHAPTER 31

Upon their return to Washington, D.C., both the FBI and the KGB reevaluated their investigations. The FBI decided to wait for any information that would come through state DMV records and the KGB decided to wait for any information that would come through the records of the Social Security Administration. With his last report to Commander Pavlovich, Kerensky had to admit the Nicola boy had gotten away and he had no more lies he could rely on to save face. He was ordered back to Moscow on the next flight out of Washington, D.C. to meet with the KGB head and his deputy commanders. He knew this meant trouble for him.

Harley and Alex spent the rest of the day on the process of washing, epoxy scrubbing and then waxing the weed sprayed cars. Harley got back to some of his normal repairs and toward late afternoon, he checked on his new employee. Alex had finished with one car and was working on another.

Harley looked at the car Alex had just cleaned and liked what he saw. He told the boy he was doing a good job but should plan on quitting soon because he was closing the shop at 6 p.m.

"How about having dinner with me at my place?" asked Harley.

Alex smiled and said, "Yeah, sure. That'd be great."

"Well let's start picking up and get cleaned up, it's about time to close."

He followed Harley to his home and upon arriving, Harley got right to fixing a pot of Mulligan stew. He asked Harley if he could watch some television and Harley told him to go ahead. After the stew was on the stove and cooking, Harley went to a pantry at the rear of the kitchen and pulled out some bottles.

He turned to Alex and proclaimed, "I'm having a little drink before dinner, Jimmy. Would you like one?"

Alex looked up from the TV and said, "Ah, a, well, no, no thanks, I don't drink."

Harley looked at him for a moment. "Not even a beer once in a while?" queried Harley.

"A, no sir, never tried any kind of alcohol."

"Well, what do you like to drink, then, I got some pop?"

"Well, sir, I like Dr. Pepper."

"Dr. Pepper?" said Harley in a rather questioning tone.

"Yes, sir, Dr. Pepper." Harley went to his refrigerator and retrieved a bottle of Dr. Pepper, popped the cap on it and handed it to Alex.

"How about that!" exclaimed Harley. "Dr. Pepper is my favorite, too. Favorite pop, that is. You sure you're not a Texan? You know Dr. Pepper is brewed right here in Texas…Dublin, Texas over south of Ft. Worth."

Alex answered, "Really, I guess I didn't know that."

Harley mixed himself an E&J VSOP brandy Manhattan, adding a dash of cherry juice. He sat down at the kitchen table across from Alex. They sat there in silence, looking at each other, while taking sips of their drinks.

He looked at Alex and said, "You're a bit of a mystery, son. You don't talk much, but that's okay. I'm glad you showed up and can help me out."

Alex blushed and took another drink of his Dr. Pepper. Harley started telling how he got into the auto repair business, emphasizing he didn't like to work on foreign cars. He chuckled when he related he sorta made an exception for the town's Chief of Police. He said he'd done some repairs on his car, a puce colored Mazda that used to belong to the chief's mother.

"Puce?" declared Alex. "Did you say his car is puce?"

"Yep, that's what I said, puce," and they both chuckled.

Harley got up to check his stew, stirred it a little and sat back down. "Okay son, what about you?" Hesitantly, Alex repeated the story he was abandoned by his mother and left on the steps of an orphanage. He went on to tell a little about his growing up. He made up a few incidental things as he talked, but nothing significant. He said authorities made some efforts to find his real parents, but after a couple of years, they basically gave up.

"You think you may try yourself, someday? Find your folks, that is?" asked Harley.

Alex quickly looked up at Harley. He was momentarily confused, caught up in his own lie. "Oh, a, no, not really." He looked back at the TV. Harley sensed the boy's hesitation.

Alex turned back and not wanting to leave the conversation on his parents, started telling Harley that after he left the orphanage, he worked at a deli. He was a dishwasher for a few months, but the hours were limited and he couldn't make enough money to pay his rent. One day he overheard two guys at the deli talking about Texas where men were needed to work in the oil fields. A few days later, he quit the dishwashing job, packed what few things he had and headed west.

Finally the stew was ready and Alex thought it was delicious. Harley had some hard rolls to go with it. They talked and laughed about how they met and how they both liked Dr. Pepper. For dessert Harley served large bowls of Maple Nut ice cream. They both laughed when he told Harley it was his all-time favorite flavor. They were starting to feel comfortable with each other's company and as they talked, Alex started thinking about maybe staying in Lake City for a while.

CHAPTER 32

The next day, Harley put up a, "Back in a few minutes," sign on the garage's office door and took Alex to the police station so he could meet his good friend, Jim Travis, the Chief of Police. Travis came to Lake City a few years ago after spending most of his law enforcement career with the Los Angeles Police Department. He picked Lake City because his mother lived there and he wanted to get back to fishing and ease into retirement in a few years.

His ex-wife Abigal, or Abby as he calls her, lives in Los Angeles and is into psychic phenomena, tarot cards, séances, and other weird stuff. A product of the hippie generation, she grew up in San Francisco, and eventually moved to LA where she met Travis at a book store where she worked.

When Travis moved to Lake City, he ended up renting a trailer home at the Lakeview Trailer Park. The trailer was owned by Pearl Adams, who was also the park manager. The owner of the park and the town's mayor was Charlie Applegate. The successful solution of the kidnapping of Applegate's granddaughter and her safe return was the first major case Travis had after arriving in town.

Pearl, a 60 something year old, soon became good friends with Travis which eventually developed into a discreet sexual relationship. At the same time this was happening, Travis was being pursued by Pearl's 38 year old daughter and Police Matron, Valerie, which also became sexual in nature.

And then there was Twyla Johnson, a 25 year old neighbor to Travis. She was a stripper at, "Boobies," a night club located a few miles outside of town. She had a solid, well-proportioned body, thanks to the regular dancing routines. She also had ample breasts and enjoyed men's stares and ogling, including catching Jim Travis occasionally glancing at them.

Twyla often admired Travis's physique and didn't hesitate to tell him as often as she could. Through her continuous and unrelenting efforts, she eventually got Travis into bed, leading to an occasional romp in the sack. Travis worried one of the three would find out about the others, however that didn't happen, but he feared the day was coming.

Travis and Harley became good friends not only through Harley working on Travis's puce colored Mazda, but Harley was quite helpful to Travis and the police in several police matters over the last couple of years. Travis also keeps Harley supplied with VSOP Brandy in part payment for the repairs he's done and helping the police.

Since Travis took over as chief, he had several major crime matters besides the kidnapping of the mayor's six year old granddaughter. His department had been directly or significantly involved with several federal agencies, identifying a local thief, an embezzler, an extortion plot and a murderer who came to town to kill Travis. Travis only had one other officer, Woody Denson through most of these problems, but got the okay to hire another officer about a year ago.

Woody Denson was a young, eager-beaver type, whose first job out of the State's Law Enforcement Academy was with the Lake City PD. He is married, wife Shirley, and they have no children. Woody was pretty prejudiced against women police officers, especially, black women police officers, until the department hired it's third officer, Hatshepsut Phoebe Jones, aka "Hattie." Woody relished working with the Feds and it was hard for him to go back to routine matters handled by the department.

Hattie was an African-American woman from a strong Christian family in Houston. The Lake City Police Department job was, like Woody Denson, her first job right out of the Texas Law Enforcement Training Academy. It didn't take her long to diffuse Denson's prejudices, actually finding out after they met, they were distant cousins. She hit the ground running and immediately got involved in helping in the solution of some of the recent crimes. She really made a name for herself when she took on and beat the crap out of a drunk one night at Boobies.

CHAPTER 33

When Harley and Alex walked into the police department, Travis was standing in Val's office. "I want you to meet Jimmy Smith," declared Harley. "He's from back east and was passing through on his way out to the oil fields. I'm putting him to work for a couple of weeks cleaning up those cars that got sprayed by the railroad."

Travis reached to shake Jimmy's hand and offered, "Welcome to Lake City, I'm Jim Travis." He turned to look at Val and said, "This is our police secretary and matron, Valerie Adams."

Jimmy shook her hand and she said, "Nice to meet you." Hearing conversation going on in the normally quiet police station, Woody and Hattie came out of their offices and approached the group. Travis, gesturing with his hand toward Woody and Hattie introduced them to Jimmy and repeated the short explanation Harley gave of why Jimmy was in Lake City. After a few minutes of, "welcomes," and "glad to meet you," Harley and Jimmy returned to the shop and Jimmy resumed working on the cars.

The sex life of Jim Travis had taken a hiatus over the last few months. He had to start turning down offers for lunch, dinner, picnics, watching TV and outright offers to have sex. He did this willingly but with some reluctance. However, he knew each of the three women he was taking to bed did not know about the others but eventually they would find out. Then what?

Although he was in his mid-50s, he maintained a solid, almost athletic build. He did some light calisthenics several times a week and tried to do some hiking when the weather permitted. With his sex life in abatement, Jim had time to fish on Lake Sherwood in his used boat and motor he purchased the previous year. He also did a little golfing and spent time on the stamp collection he inherited from his father. He was also starting to spend more time with his mother, Gladys Travis. She was nearing 90 years of age and lived in her own apartment, within walking distance of the Lakeview Trailer Park.

It was her Mazda that Jim drove. She gave it to him, after she decided she didn't want to drive anymore. She was a very wary woman for her age and had alerted her son several times, helping in the solution of some of the police matters. She also had a network of card playing ladies, which helped her keep track of most everyone in Lake City.

After meeting Jimmy Smith, well, not the real Jimmy Smith, Hattie returned to her small office cubicle. Since she was the last one hired, she got the only remaining space available in the department. Val had the front office next to the front door so she could greet anyone entering the police department.

Woody had a slightly bigger office and the chief, had an office across the main room of the building where he could also see anyone entering through the front door, and also see into Val's office. There were a few chairs in the middle of the room and a small table with a coffee pot and cups against the wall. In the back there were two jail cells and next to them were the restrooms.

Now Hattie was far from what one would describe as "svelte." She was 24 years old, 5'6" and 225 pounds. She had to squeeze her way in and out of her desk chair. This was her first job as a police officer and she was excited, because her boyfriend, Raymond Charles Owens, aka, "Whimpy," was moving from Houston to Lake City in a week.

He was hired by the new manager of The Dollar General Store, who took over when the previous manager went to jail for embezzlement. The new manager, Jupiter Jones, no relation to Hattie, was transferred to the Lake City store, from the Longview, Texas store where he was the assistant manager.

Lake City only had a few African-American residents. A few eyebrows were raised and there was some talk when Hattie was hired and moved to town. Now they had another black resident in Jupiter Jones. This time if there were eyebrows raised, no one seemed to be concerned. Perhaps due to the Lake City Journal's article about Mr. Jones, with pictures of he and his family. The family consisted of his wife, a daughter in the junior grades and a 6'5" son, a junior in high school.

The article went on to report the son was an all-state basketball player as a sophomore at Longview. You see, Lake City had a little reputation as a basketball town, and adding a 6'5" all-state player to the high school team had everyone smiling, checking the upcoming basketball schedule and starting to brag about how good the team was going to be this year.

Anyway, Mr. Jones did indeed hire Hattie's high school boyfriend, Whimpy. Hattie called him, "Ray." Raymond Charles Owens was a black man that weighed 125 lbs. He and Hattie made a nice pair. Hattie sat and thought about

Ray moving to town and living with her in her apartment. *Maybe we'll settle down and get married. Oh, wouldn't that be nice. And maybe start to think about a family!* She came out of her thoughts when family came to mind. She told herself she had to call her mom tonight after work. Hattie was from a large family of all girls, who as early as she could remember, went to church every Sunday.

Val came into Hattie's office and laid some reports on her desk. "Thank you," uttered Hattie as Val turned and headed back to her office. Hattie looked at Val's figure in envy. Val and her mother Pearl were tall with olive colored skin and very nice figures. They were Native Americans from a tribe in North Dakota that had intermarried with French trappers years ago. Neither one was married nor seemed to date much, as far as Hattie knew.

Woody Denson was 26 years old and had settled into the normal, mostly boring police work in Lake City. He grew up in Concan, Texas, in the hill country, and had finally gotten over the disappointment that his best friend growing up was charged and sentenced for fraud. He stayed with Woody and his wife for a while until his "business tactics," caught up with him. Oh, there had been enough excitement to keep Woody's interest over the last couple of years. He especially liked working with the Feds who got involved in the kidnapping and mail fraud investigations that took place since he was hired.

Although he was initially vehemently opposed to hiring a black female officer, he and Hattie actually hit it off and had become good friends. Woody and his wife, Shirley had Hattie over for dinner at least once a week and when her boyfriend was in town, they would have them both over for dinner. Outside of his job, Woody didn't have any hobbies or outside interests other than watching movies on television. Shirley was also a movie fan, but also did sewing and quilting as a hobby.

CHAPTER 34

Chief Travis spent most of the day going over monthly reports and planning to meet with the city council in a couple of days for their usual monthly report of police activities. Travis wasn't much into statistics, but the incidents of police matters and intervention in Lake City was not all that much, so he didn't mind the council meetings. He planned to leave work a little early that day. He wanted to check out a rattle under his Mazda and if there was a problem, would have to get it to Harley to be fixed.

He told Val he was leaving and drove the 10 minute drive to his trailer. He parked the police car next to the Mazda and as he stopped to check his mailbox, heard someone holler, "Jim, hey Jim." He looked up and saw his neighbor Twyla Johnson in her front yard holding a garden tool. She was waving at him to come over, so he headed her way. "Hi Jim," she said with a big smile and her eyes fixed on him. He felt a slight "melt down," as he always did when she gave him that look.

Travis was very familiar with that look and some quick flashes of some of their previous sexual encounters came to mind. She was talking to him and he missed the first part of whatever she was saying. ".....full sun or partial?" He looked at her and saw she was holding several small flower plants and was looking at him for an answer.

"Ah, a, ah, gee Twyla I really don't know."

"Well, the guy at the store told me he thought they needed full sun, but I wanted to plant them here in the front where there isn't full sun." She was braless and Travis had trouble not looking at her breasts.

A 26 year old dancer, she kept a very curvy, well-built shape. He wanted to change the subject, so asked her about a recent incident at Boobies. He heard there was a scuffle between two guys, but the Sheriff's Office didn't respond. She told him no one got hurt and she never saw the guys before. As she squatted down to plant the flowers, Travis seemed satisfied with her explanation and said, "Well I got to go. Have to check on a rattle under my car. See you later."

"Okay, Jim, bye," and he headed back to his trailer.

The next six days went well for Alex. Harley started paying him daily for cleaning the cars and Alex had a chance to get to know a few more townspeople. One was Travis's Mother, Gladys. She stopped into the shop one day after hearing from her son about Harley's new helper. Now Gladys was not really what you'd call the nosy type, however, she liked the idea she knew everyone in town and oftentimes bragged about it. So, when she heard about the young man in town, she wanted to meet him.

Harley took Gladys to the rear of the shop where Alex

was working on the cars. "Jimmy, I want you to meet someone." Jimmy looked up from a half cleaned hub cap he'd been working on and wiping his hands greeted the woman with Harley.

"Hello, young man. I'm Gladys, Gladys Travis."

Jimmy reached out to shake her hand and smiling said, "Hi, I'm, a, Jimmy, Jimmy Smith."

"I'm certainly glad to meet you, Jimmy Smith. How do you like Lake City?" He smiled and glanced at Harley who was looking from him to Gladys and then back as each said something.

"I like it. Met some real nice people and Harley here has been very kind to me." They both looked at Harley who looked down to the ground and blushed.

Gladys liked the boy immediately. He was well-mannered and had a nice smile. When her son told her about Jimmy and how he was raised in an orphanage, she had commented, "Oh, that poor boy."

"What are your plans, Jimmy? I hear you want to work in the oil fields, that right?" asked Gladys.

"Well, a, ah, I guess that's where I'll head when I leave here."

"Well why not stay here, here in Lake City? My friend, Helen Humsoffen has a son who manages the elevator and she said he's looking for a couple of drivers to help with the spring harvest."

"Well, I don't know, Mrs. Travis. I appreciate the tip, though, thanks."

"Okay, Jimmy. You think about it. We'd be happy to have you as a resident and I'm going to have you and Harley over for dinner one of these nights, real soon, okay?"

"Oh, yeah, that's sounds good, doesn't it Harley?"

"Sure does. Gladys is well known in these parts for her cooking."

"Well, I better let you get back to work. I'll let you know about dinner."

Harley and Alex both muttered, "Okays," as she turned and walked away.

A few days later, Gladys did have Jimmy, Harley and

her son Jim all over for pot roast, potatoes and gravy, carrots, salad and strawberry-rhubarb pie a la mode. That was how things went for Jimmy over the next week or so until he started working on the last car to be cleaned. Harley wanted to keep the boy on as a helper, but couldn't really afford him, even though the boy seemed to like staying in the repair shop office.

CHAPTER 35

One day, Jimmy mentioned to Harley he was going to work on his stamp collection that evening. Harley told him Jim Travis was also a stamp collector and occasionally goes to one of the stamp shows in the area. Jimmy made a mental note to talk to Travis about his collection and felt a slight, "kinship," to Travis just knowing he collected stamps.

Also into stamps, was FBI Special Agent Willis Emerson. He learned in records found when county officials inventoried the Nicola home, that Alex had purchased some Russian stamps on several occasions from a stamp store in Hoboken, New Jersey. This was one of many leads the FBI was working on in efforts to locate Alex. Emerson sent a communication to the Hoboken Office of the FBI requesting agents contact the owner of Euro-Russia Stamps, 555 Central Parkway in Hoboken to see if Alex ordered any stamps recently. If he hadn't, they were to ask the store owner to notify them immediately if he heard anything from Alex Nicola, or a Jimmy Smith.

Meanwhile, at the Russian Embassy in Washington, D.C., Major General Boris Kerensky had survived his ordered return to Moscow to face his Commander and a panel of his generals. Kerensky and his agents resumed their efforts to determine the location of the young Nicola boy. Analyst Gagari Putin was under orders to check twice a day with his fiancée, Anna Bukhart, at the Social Security Office in Washington.

Twice a day, Putin reported back to his boss that Anna had still not found any new entries for James Alan Smith. They also tried to make an informant out of a young man working for the District's Motor Vehicle Department, but he reported the contact to the FBI, who responded with a letter to the embassy threatening the Soviets with expulsions for harassing an American citizen.

The last day Alex would be cleaning cars for Harley, he decided he would apply for a truck driver's job at the elevator. He was getting to like Lake City and only occasionally gave any thought about the FBI or Russians trying to find him. He was feeling pretty safe. Maybe if he got the elevator job and saved some money he would move on later.

Harley told him he could stay at the office at night for as long as he wanted, but he thought he'd try to find an apartment if he found another job. He would go talk to the guy at the elevator that afternoon since he would soon be finished with the last car. He also wanted to stop in to see the police chief and mention to him about being a stamp collector. Alex decided to do that right after he applied for the elevator job.

His experience at the mining company in Beckley paid

off for Alex. The elevator manager had heard about the young orphan lad who came to town and, after looking over his application and talking to him about the job, decided to hire him. He would be driving a grain truck from the fields to the elevator.

Farmers would soon be busy with the soybean harvest and several had to hire the elevator to help with transporting the beans to the elevator. It would only be about a three or four week job, but the manager mentioned if things worked out well, he may have another job for Alex at the elevator.

Elated he found another job, he drove to the police station to see Chief Travis. When he entered the station, Val told him the chief was on the phone and asked him to have a seat. Travis was talking to his ex-wife Abby.

"But Abby, I don't know about this. It's awfully sudden and I guess I'd have to think about it." Abigal and Travis met at a Los Angeles book store, got married and lived fairly happily until she started getting into psychic phenomena, tarot cards and attending séances in trying to make contact with her deceased parents. That and his hours as a police officer eventually led to a divorce. After he moved to Lake City, they maintained a, "phone friendly," relationship and he even stayed at her apartment a couple of times when he was back in town.

Abby lost her job at the book store when it closed but was not overly upset it. It gave her the chance to attend a LA area Remote Viewing Laboratory, studying psychic intelligence. Being a somewhat restless spirit, she was now ready to move on to something else, but was having trouble finding another job. Her phone call to Travis was a request to move to Lake City and temporarily stay with him. She was broke and needed a little time to get back on her feet.

"Oh, come on, Jim. We could just see how it works out. It wouldn't be permanent and only till I save a little money."

"But people are going to talk and what do you think mother would say?" Jim replied. He was also thinking about the three women in town who he had taken to bed.

What kind of a problem would that cause?

"Jim, I'm not asking to get remarried or reestablishing our relationship. I just need to find a little job. Maybe even a part-time one and it would only be for probably a few months. Besides I've got a couple of girl friends here who will be keeping their eyes open in case something opens up I could do. If that happens, then I'm out of there and back to LA."

"Abby, I've got someone waiting to see me," said Travis looking up and seeing Jimmy Smith waiting for him.

"Let's both think about this for a few days and I'll call you, maybe this weekend, okay?"

"Okay, Jim. Thanks." He heard a click on the other end of the line, so he hung up. As he arose to walk out of his office he thought, *Abby and me living together, in my trailer!* Jimmy stood up when Travis walked up. They greeted each other and Travis invited him back to his office.

Jimmy told Travis he wanted to talk to him because Harley told him Travis also was a stamp collector. Travis acknowledged the comment, smiled and nodded his head.

Jimmy related how he started collecting as a young boy at the orphanage. He told Travis the orphanage received a lot of donated stamps and one time the donation was mostly Russian stamps and he's had a Russian collection ever since.

Travis explained to Jimmy he'd inherited his father's collection and liked to spend quiet evenings sorting and mounting stamps into his albums. They talked about stamp shows, dealers and other sources of getting stamps. Travis told him he liked to go to stamp shows, especially the one every November near Dallas at Grapevine, Texas.

Val appeared at the door of the chief's office and told him he had a call. Jimmy shook his hand and they agreed to get together some evening and look at each other's stamp collections. Jimmy exited the station feeling pretty good. He had a job, a place to stay, and now someone he could share his stamp collecting hobby with. As he walked back to Harley's Repair Shop, he felt the best he'd felt since leaving Silver Springs. That was about to change for young Alex, aka James Alan Smith.

CHAPTER 36

It was several days later that Travis returned the call to his ex-wife, Abby. He put it off as long as he could and was expecting her to call him back, real soon. He had given a lot of thought to their sharing his small trailer. Deep down, he realized he was still very fond of her. Maybe even still in love? It would only be temporary and he told himself they would both have to agree to that aspect. However, it certainly would put a damper on his relationships with Pearl, Val and Twyla. And, what would the people in town say? He finally decided he could tell everyone they were trying a reconciliation, everyone would surely be open to that, wouldn't they? Then, after Abby went back to LA, maybe he could resume seeing the three women?

"Hi Abby," he said when she answered.

"Oh, hi Jim. How are you?"

"I'm fine, Abby. Look, I've given this thing about you moving here a lot of thought."

"Yes," she uttered in a tone of anticipation.

"If we can agree it's only temporary, no more than three months, then I guess it'd be okay. Would you agree to that?"

"Sure, Jim. I understand. It's just that right now I've run out of money. I'm sure I can find something there and remember I have several girl friends here all looking for a job for me."

Abby went on to tell him one of her friends said she could store her furniture in her garage. She told Travis she would start packing and drive out to Lake City by the end of the month. After they hung up, Jim looked at the calendar and felt somewhat relieved. He had a couple of weeks to prepare for her arrival.

The next two weeks went by quickly, both for Jim Travis and Jimmy Smith. Travis started the process of moving some things into the trailer's storage shed. Jimmy started his new job at the elevator and was happy to be working some overtime hours, too.

Pearl Adams heard from her daughter, Val that Jim Travis's ex-wife was moving to town and going to live with him. Pearl was a little saddened by the news. She always had in the back of her mind she and Jim would become an item, maybe even marry someday. Her thoughts that morning kept going back to her and Jim making love, thoughts interrupted from time to time as she tried to send out the monthly rental statements. She decided she would do everything possible to make love to him at least one more time before his ex arrived.

Val was probably the most crushed by the news of Abby's arrival. Nearing 40, she wanted to start a family and dreamed of it being with her boss, Jim Travis. She made a vow to keep him as a lover. As she sat there watching television and thought about her future, a plan started forming in her head.

Twyla Johnson was probably the least concerned about Abby's arrival. Oh, she certainly would miss the sex she and Jim always enjoyed. She sat in her trailer, having several hours before she had to report for work that evening. Her thoughts were all of Jim and she could see his nude, muscular body in her mind. *What if Jim's ex makes Lake City her permanent home?* As she sat there thinking about the situation, suddenly an idea popped into her head and a slowly developing smile came to life.

The power of the female psyche would be one way to describe how the following events took place all within the last five days prior to Abby Travis's arrival at Lake City. Through those several days, Pearl, Val and Twyla were each able to conjure up a scheme to lure, entice or trick Jim Travis into getting in bed with them. Pearl used her wonderful cooking skills and went all out for a prime rib dinner and all the trimmings, followed by strawberry-rhubarb pie, putting Jim on a guilt trip he hadn't had for years. They made love slowly, tenderly and reached new heights of pleasure that night.

For Val, she used the power of alcohol, specifically Jim's fondness for brandy manhattans. There was no dinner involved in this tryst. She basically doubled the amount of brandy in the drink she fixed for him that evening. She sipped a pinot noir and watched him as he tried to reset her cable channels on the television. Cable channels she intentionally screwed up that morning before going to work.

Jim, being the helpful sole he was, succumbed to Val's pleading to come over after work to help her with her TV. Her low cut tank top had not gone unnoticed by Jim as he struggled with trying to figure out how the channels were so screwed up. When she bent over to see what he was doing, he looked up and into her now sagging blouse. Her ample breasts were now in full view and her face was a few inches from his face. As she was looking into his eyes with a mischievous smile on her face, she leaned forward and kissed him. He dropped the remote and cords, picked her up and carried her into the bedroom. They never got back to trying to sort out the TV problem, which Val fixed the next morning before leaving for work.

For Twyla, it was by doing something she always wanted to do in front of Jim. Being a stripper came very naturally to her and she actually liked the thought that she could "turn men on." That night, at her trailer, that's exactly what she did to poor, old unsuspecting Jim Travis. She waved at him one early evening as he was ending his walk. When he approached her trailer she told him she had a new CD and wanted him to hear it. She put on a recording of "Bolero," and catching him off guard, started the best strip she had ever done. When the song ended, Jim sat in a stupor. She replayed it, removing the rest of her clothes just as it finished the second time. In her previous sex with him, he made love to her slow and deliberate. This time it was over almost before they got started.

CHAPTER 37

Other than those sexual adventures, the rest of the events in Lake City and for the Lake City Police Department went by quietly. Hattie Jones did arrest a panhandler who was passing through and when she stopped to question him about soliciting money from the townspeople, he called her a nigger and she decided a night in jail might do him some good. The next day she gave him a few bucks to catch the bus to Dallas, after the City Attorney decided to not file any charges.

With several weeks' pay and an advance from the elevator manager, Alex was able to rent one of the vacant apartments above the Jalapeño Café. Just down the hall, Hattie, the police woman, and her fiancé Whimpy, shared an apartment.

Abigal Travis arrived in Lake City late one sunny afternoon in her used, and slightly abused, Subaru station wagon. It was packed so full you couldn't see out the side or back windows. There were boxes and tote containers tied down to the roof rack with clothesline rope. She stopped at the police station and met all the people she had heard Jim talk about; Woody, Val and Hattie. Jim took off a little early that afternoon to show Abby how to get to his trailer and help her start to unpack.

Later that week, Alex took out a catalog from a stamp dealer in Hoboken, New Jersey and started a list of Russian stamps he needed and might want to order. A week later he finished the list. He mailed the list and a money order to the dealer.

A week after that, the first withholding information

reached the Social Security Administration offices in Baltimore for James Alan Smith and his employment with the Lake City Farmers Elevator, Lake City, Texas.

The stamp dealer in Hoboken filled Alex's order for all but one of the Russian stamps and wrote out a refund certificate on future purchases. He mailed off the stamps to "Jimmy Smith" in Lake City, Texas and filed the order list in his records. He had forgotten about the visit from the FBI. It was approximately two weeks later while watching a law enforcement TV show, the FBI was mentioned. That reminded him of the FBI's request and he made a mental note to call them the next day.

Due to a government furlough over the federal budget in Congress, nonessential employees of most all of the government agencies ordered their employees to take off one day a week, till the crisis was resolved. This included the Social Security Administration and therefore it was three more weeks before the filing of earnings for James Alan Smith reached Anna Bukhart's department in Washington, D.C.

Things continued to go well for Alex in Lake City. He was settling in more and more to a nice quiet lifestyle and was enjoying the people, his job and having his own apartment. He and Jim Travis had gotten together several times to show each other their stamp collections and do some trading. Travis's collection didn't have as many Russian issues as Jimmy's, but the more Russian stamps he got from Jimmy, the more interested he became in that country's culture and history.

During these visits, all at Alex's apartment, Travis was getting to know Jimmy a little better. He was able to get Jimmy to talk more and more about his life growing up in an orphanage. By now, Jimmy's orphanage story had become fairly well known. He had repeated it often enough, he was now comfortable with even expanding on it some.

One evening, Jimmy inadvertently said something about Russian relatives. When Jim questioned him about it, Jimmy back pedaled and stammered a little with, "Well, a, not that I know for sure, ah, ah, but I always suspected my mother or father, you know, and maybe it was something someone said one time at the orphanage, I don't know." Travis let it drop but did think about it later and sensed something about Jimmy Smith he wasn't quite sure about.

A couple of days later, Travis ran into Harley coming back from breakfast and after a few moments of idle chat, Travis asked him, "Harley what's your take on Jimmy Smith?"

Harley studied Jim's face and finally said, "Well, he sure seems like a nice enough kid, I guess. Why do you ask?"

"Well, he said something the other night about his relatives and I got the impression it slipped out by mistake. He ever say anything to you about having any Russian relatives?"

"No, not that I remember," replied Harley. "He told me he thought his mother came over from Russia to work for a Senator or government official."

"Yeah, it just sounded a little suspicious. I don't know. Forget about it, it was probably nothing."

"Okay," said Harley and they parted with both saying,

"See ya later."

CHAPTER 38

One night, Twyla dreamt she was pregnant. She awoke with a start and checked her calendar. She was two and half months late with her menstrual cycle. She got back into bed and started wondering what was going on. The only sex she had was with Jim Travis and she always used a condom. *I can't be pregnant, could I?* She got to thinking maybe she had been a little tired lately. But she never missed her period before. She made a note to go see a doctor.

That very same morning, Val Adams was looking at her

calendar. *Let's see, it's been two and a half months,* looking at a small little check mark on the date she and Travis last had sex. She had a warm, dreamy feeling that morning as she started to think about becoming a mother. She had a secret she could never share with anyone. Just her secret between her and the baby, she felt sure was growing inside her. It only took a little pin prick at the end of the condom. Jim had no idea and no one would ever know about her plan, a plan to become the mother of Jim Travis's baby.

Two days later, Shirley Denson was busy in her kitchen doing the morning dishes when she suddenly had an urge to throw up. She ran into the bathroom but the urge went away. She went back to her dishes. As she finished drying the last cup, it dawned on her she was feeling a little tired. She hadn't stayed up late the night before. She and Woody went to bed right after the 10 o'clock news. Over the next few days, Shirley didn't have much of an appetite and found the smell of food caused her to feel sick.

When she was talking to her mother one day, she mentioned she was feeling tired lately and had lost her appetite. Her mother said her, "Sounds to me like you're pregnant." Her menstrual cycle had always been very irregular so she never really kept track of it. But checking her calendar, she saw her last period had been three months ago. She decided to go see Dr. Martin and not say anything to Woody.

It may have been something in the air? Well, maybe not, but also on that morning, as she was getting dressed for work, Hatshepsut Phoebe Jones realized she'd missed her last two periods. Since she and Ray had become sexually active, she had been on the pill. She wondered what was going on. Had she forgotten to take one of her pills? She didn't think so, but having always been very regular with her period, she decided she better get it checked. She planned to call for a doctor's appointment later that day.

CHAPTER 39

The stamp dealer at Hoboken apologized to the FBI Agent on the phone. He told the agent he did get an order from a Jimmy Smith and took a few minutes to pull out the order. The agent wrote down the address and the date of the order. He thanked the dealer and cautioned him to not say anything to anyone about the matter. The agent headed for his supervisor's office. After hearing the details, the supervisor called WFO and asked to speak to the Foreign Intelligence Supervisor.

It was exactly one week later that Anna Bukhart saw the

earnings statement information for James Alan Smith. With no one looking, she pulled out a small pad and jotted down the submitting business, “Lake City Farmers Elevator, Lake City, Texas.” At her break, she phoned her fiancé, Gagari. He was so pleased with the information; he told her he would take her to dinner that evening. Then he quickly hung up and rushed to Piotr Blok’s office.

Blok told Putin to come with him to Kerensky’s office. When they got to his office, his secretary told them he was out for several hours and expected back by 4 p.m. He was “out,” all right, out with the same two hookers he was now seeing at least twice a week. He didn’t come back to the embassy until 6 p.m., and when he walked to his office, several thought he looked a little frazzled.

Abby did get a job in Lake City. She was hired as a cashier at the Dollar General store by the manager, Juniper Jones. Her previous experience in retail and the need for someone to keep an eye on the cashiers, was just what Jones wanted. With the weather turning cooler, she and Jim started going on evening walks. They also liked getting some needed exercise. She slept on his couch and he in his bedroom, and, "neither the twain did meet." He kept busy at work and was now spending at least two evenings a week with Jimmy Smith working on their stamp collections.

Lake City had only one pediatrician, Dr. Joseph Martin. Now in his early 80's, he was known far and wide, because he delivered most every resident in and around Lake City. It was a Friday morning and his waiting room was filled with four people, three expectant mothers and one with a small three-month old.

Val went to Dr. Martin's office early that day. The office was two blocks off Main Street on Second Avenue. The same location he'd had for years. After signing in, she took a seat. As she waited for her turn to see the doctor, Val had visions of all the wonderful chores involved with raising a child. She could see herself, the baby and Jim Travis walking the streets of Lake City showing off the beautiful infant. Val glanced around the waiting room. She only recognized one other expectant woman, the wife of the man who owned and operated the Jalapeno Café. The woman looked up as Val glanced her way, and she gave Val a slight smile and returned to her magazine.

Then a skinny teenage girl entered the waiting room, checked in and took a seat. Val didn't know her and was a little startled at the age of the girl and it looked like she was due any day. A few minutes later, the door opened and in walked Hattie. She stopped in her tracks when she saw Val. Val was staring at Hattie. Hattie was staring at Val. The other women were looking back and forth at Val and Hattie, like heads at a tennis match.

"Hattie?" blurted out Val, in a questioning tone.

"Val?" Hattie responded. There was only silence as all kinds of thoughts were obviously running through both of their minds. Hattie was there to get something to get her back to regular cycles and get on with her life. Maybe Val was there for the same reason? But the flushed, embarrassed look on Val's face told it all and Hattie had a pretty good idea why Val was there.

As Hattie was finishing checking in with the

receptionist, the waiting room door opened again and in walked Twyla Johnson. Both Val and Hattie's jaws dropped. Twyla was so surprised to see them she forgot where she was or why she was there. She greeted them the same as she would if she saw them on the street.

"Good morning, Val. Good morning Hattie, how are you?" Now Val and Hattie looked at each other and then back at Twyla. There was so much "what if's and why's," going through the three ladies heads that you could almost see wisps of smoke rising over their heads from over worked brain cells.

Thinking she didn't need an appointment, Woody's wife Shirley decided to pop into Dr. Martin's office for a quick checkup. She was sure he would say she wasn't pregnant and that would be that. She was very surprised when she came into the doctor's waiting room. Why, it was almost full of women. It took her a moment or two to realize she knew three of them; Val, Twyla and Hattie. They all looked up when she entered the room and then each looked at each other in disbelief.

Twyla was seated across from Val who had moved to a seat next to Hattie. After signing in, Shirley sat down next to Twyla. They all had questioning looks on their faces and just kept looking at each other. None of them knew what to say. Finally a slight smirk started developing on Val's face, the other's saw it and they all started giggling and laughing.

Now the women knew Hattie was living with Whimpy and they were engaged to be married. They also knew Val dated a few guys from time to time, but they didn't know about her and Jim Travis. As for Twyla, they were aware she was a stripper and probably met lots of men. Maybe she met someone at her club they didn't know about. And none of them were surprised to see Shirley there, but it was just the timing of it all that got to them and the giggling continued.

Four days later two of them found out they were indeed pregnant and two were informed they weren't. Twyla and Val were told the doctor had written prescriptions for them to help regulate their menstrual cycles. Twyla had only slept with Jim Travis and was warming up to the idea of being Mrs. Travis. But after the call from the doctor's office, she quickly put aside any more thoughts of marrying him and having his baby.

Val was heart-broken with the news. She received the doctor's call late one afternoon at the police station. She was in a semi-shock since she had planned things so well. She felt so bad she went into Travis's office and told him she didn't feel well and was going home. She immediately turned and walked out of the station. Travis didn't have a chance to say anything and just watched as she left. She called in sick the next morning and, needing to tell someone about her grief, called her mother and told her she wanted to come over and talk to her about something.

Shirley could hardly wait till Woody got home that evening. She fixed steak, potatoes and gravy, and asparagus for dinner. Half-way through the meal she told him the news. He looked up quickly and then jumped up and shouted out, "Yes!" grabbed his wife and started dancing her around the room.

Hattie was the one in the most shock to learn she was pregnant. She had faithfully taken her pills and now with her career just starting, she wasn't ready to have it interrupted by having a baby. When Raymond Charles Owens later heard the news, he started jumping around and clapping his hands. He was totally elated. He grabbed Hattie and kissed her, then he danced some more. He interrupted his dancing glee by kissing her again. She just stood there and stared at his antics. He obviously was way more joyous about the news than she was.

CHAPTER 40

FBI Agents Willis Emerson III and Joseph W. Brewer were told by their supervisor to get to Lake City as soon as possible by taking the next plane to Dallas. They would be met by fellow agents assigned to the Dallas Office and be provided a Bureau vehicle and two back-up units. Their orders were to find Alexander Nicola, warn and convince him the Russians were going to kill him. They were to again offer him protection under the government's Witness Protection Program.

When Kerensky got the news that employment

information had come in for Alexander Nicola, using James Alan Smith, in Lake City, Texas, he summoned his two best agents, one a sniper expert. His orders were very simple, "Find the boy and kill him." The two flew out of Washington National Airport for Dallas, Texas that night. Kerensky was relieved and elated to finally end the saga of the search for Alex. He buzzed Yakov and told him to contact the two prostitutes. He wanted to spend the night with them and meet as soon as possible at the usual location. He put in a call to Moscow and was told Commander Pavlovich had a bad case of diarrhea and would call him back later. Kerensky couldn't wait and took off for his all night engagement.

It was one and half hours later that Pavlovich returned Kerensky's call. The timing was lousy. He struggled to move the two women aside so he could get up to answer the phone. He finally was able to answer the phone after seven long rings. The black prostitute heard him mumble something about being in the bathroom. She heard some grunting noises and garbled talk coming from the other line. Then she heard Kerensky say something about "Lake City, Texas," and after that some other low conversation, including the name "Nicola." The conversation ended abruptly and he returned to the bedroom.

In an early morning phone call to the FBI, the prostitute told her agent contact about the call Kerensky received and what she overheard. This information was relayed to the Dallas Office of the FBI to be furnished to Agents Emerson and Brewer upon their arrival. An additional two back-up teams and the office SWAT team were ordered to help locate Alex Nicola and protect him from the Soviets.

Valerie Adams had to tell someone about her grief, and her mother, Pearl, was the only one she thought she could trust. In her mother's trailer, within eyeshot of Jim Travis's trailer, she told her mother about her plan to get pregnant with Jim Travis's baby. She started sobbing and mumbled out, "But it didn't work and I'm not pregnant." Pearl had turned an ashen white. She just stared at Val. She didn't know what to say, and even if she did, her throat felt like it was full of cotton.

Val's sobbing continued for a few more minutes. Finally, it occurred to her that her mother had not said a word and was looking very, very pale. Pearl got up, went to a small cabinet and pulled out a bottle of Jack Daniels. A bottle she was been saving for another special night with Jim Travis. It was now too late for that. She poured herself a generous portion of the whiskey, took a huge swig, then another and turned to face her daughter. She sat her glass down on the kitchen table and walked over to Val. She put her arms around her and said, "Oh Val, I'm so sorry."

Val, now calmed a bit, stood up and hugged her mom. Then she sat back down and started telling her mother all the minute details of her failed plan. Pearl took another huge gulp of her drink and all she could think of was, *and I thought I was the only one he was screwing. He was screwing Val and me and who knows who else? That son-of-a-bitch!*

Abby was starting to enjoy her move to Lake City. She and Jim had some nice, quiet dinners together and she was getting back into fixing some of their old favorite recipes. Jim, too, was getting very comfortable with the living situation. He got up early to go to work and usually was leaving about the time she got up. She enjoyed her new job and was getting to know and enjoy a few of the regular customers.

She reacquainted herself with Jim's mother, Gladys, and had her over for dinner at least once every two weeks. She and Gladys always had a great relationship and it was good reconnecting. All this started to put some thoughts into Abby's mind, thoughts about her and Jim back together again. Many nights she would lie on the couch before going to sleep and would be thinking about him, their past, their sex life and their love for each other… at one time anyway.

Abby heard the news about the pregnancies from Whimpy at Dollar General. He was going around the store telling everyone, co-workers as well as customers, he was going to be a father. He also related to Abby how Hattie ran into Twyla, Val and Shirley at the doctor's office, all thinking they were pregnant.

After she heard of the women all going to the doctor,

Abby started thinking and pondering the situation. First, she was a little shocked all four thought they were pregnant at the same time. *Shirley is married to Woody, okay. Hattie is living with Whimpy, okay. But Val and Twyla?*

Abby didn't know too much about Twyla, except she was Jim's neighbor and a stripper at a night club. *She is young and attractive. Does she have a boyfriend? Haven't seen anyone or any cars at her place since I came to town. Maybe she's doing more than dancing at the club?* Then her thoughts turned to Val. *She too, is young and attractive. But did she have a boyfriend? Jim has never said anything about her seeing anyone. She seems to be dedicated to her job at the police station. Most of the men she's around seem to be just Woody and Jim. Jim…hmm…. I wonder?*

CHAPTER 41

When Travis came home from work that evening, Abby asked him if he'd heard the news that Hattie and Shirley were expecting. He told her, "Yes, Woody and Hattie told me this morning." She didn't say anything and watched Jim as he started fixing himself a brandy Manhattan. He turned to look at her and asked her if she wanted something to drink.

She told him, "No."

As he walked by the stove, he looked into the oven, "What's for supper?"

"It's a chicken with potatoes and vegetables."

He took a seat at the kitchen table. She kept looking at him. He started going through the mail as he sipped on his drink.

"I guess Twyla and Val also thought they were pregnant," she finally added as she waited for his reaction.

"Yeah, that's what Hattie told me," as he took another sip of his drink.

"You wouldn't know anything about that, would you?"

He quickly looked up at her. "Abby, what are you trying to say?

Abby replied, "I just think it is quite a coincidence you are a close neighbor to one and work with the other." They stared at each other for a few moments. Jim turned back around to his drink, took a healthy gulp and asked her to come over and sit down.

He told her it was true he had slept with both Val and Twyla a few times and he deeply regretted it. He wasn't about to say anything about Pearl. He told Abby to pour herself a glass of wine and she did. Then he slowly related how he was seduced by both of them during late night visits to his trailer.

"Did they know you were screwing both of them?" Abby pointedly asked in a stern tone.

"No, they didn't, but I was afraid that they would, so I stopped seeing them."

"Jim, what the hell were you thinking, they could have become pregnant? Is that all you've been doing the last couple of years, going around screwing every woman you could get your hands on?"

"No, now Abby just hold on. I haven't been screwing every woman in town and I always wore a condom. I told you I'm not proud of what I did. I've even had several sessions with a church pastor."

"Yeah, well tell me another one, Casanova. I can hardly wait."

"Abby will you just stop. These women came on to me. They wanted to have sex."

She took another sip of her wine. He looked away and they sat in silence for several minutes. He knew she was upset and anything more he might say wouldn't help. Abby got up and pulled the pan from the oven. She filled a plate with food and set it on the table. She took off her apron, threw it on the table and stomped into the bedroom. He fixed himself another drink and it occurred to him he'd probably be spending the night on the sofa.

Abby's thoughts over the next two and half days went from being furious to jealousy. She started thinking of herself and the pregnant women as an exclusive group. She actually felt camaraderie toward them. All these thoughts were also working on her hormones and she started having strong desires to have sex with Jim. Part of the increased desire may have been a feeling of wanting to compete and part of it may have been feeling left out and wanted to reclaim what was rightfully hers?

CHAPTER 42

Late the next afternoon, the FBI set up a surveillance of the Lake City Farmers Elevator. Normally they would have touched base with the local law enforcement, but in this case things were moving to rapidly. Agent Emerson planned to contact them later. Their check of the elevator premises indicated no sign of the Russians so they settled in to wait. Emerson pointed out to the other agents, Alex's 1972 Impala parked off to one side of the elevator. They waited.

Shortly after 4:30 that afternoon, a grain truck came

into the main parking lot and headed for the weigh scales. It was being driven by Alexander Nicola. After a few minutes the agents noticed the truck drove out of the scales and turned right to the other side of the building.

"He's headed for another lot just to the east," was heard on the FBI radio.

"10-4," came the reply.

Alex parked the grain truck next to several other grain trucks, then walked up the few steps to the back entrance of the elevator.

"He's gone inside," one of the agents reported.

Another, "10-4," followed. At ten after five, Alex was observed walking out of the front entrance of the elevator and heading for his car. Emerson and Brewer met him as he opened his car door.

Alex was really taken by surprise. His stay in Lake City had lowered his guard and he didn't recognize the two men at first glance. They told him to get into his car. Agent Emerson got in the front and Brewer into the back. The conversation didn't go well. Alex was upset the Feds had found him and he started thinking about getting out of town. They laid it on the line.

The Russians knew of his location and would kill him. They suspected the Soviets had someone inside the Social Security Administration and would keep on his tail till they found him. Emerson again brought up protection and a new identity under the Witness Protection Program. Alex didn't like what he was hearing and he didn't like his options. He needed time to think.

"Tell me again how this protection program works," Alex murmured. Emerson told him the government would give him a new name with a birth certificate, social security number and driver's license. He would have the choice of two different locations in the U.S. and they would furnish him a place to live and help him find employment. "We've done this many times, so it's not like you're the first person to ever do this," explained Agent Emerson.

From the back seat, Brewer interjected, "It takes about three to four months for the KGB to get your employment records. We're sure you don't want to have to keep on the run and changing jobs every few months, do you?" Alex was looking down. His palms were getting sweaty and he was trying to think, but they kept talking.

Finally he muttered a "No."

After some silence, Emerson said, "Tell you what, think about it overnight and we'll meet you tomorrow morning right here in the parking lot at 8 a.m."

"Okay," said Alex, hesitantly.

The agents got out of the car and Emerson turned and repeated, "Tomorrow, 8 a.m." Alex nodded and Emerson shut the door and walked away.

CHAPTER 43

Alex sat in his car with his head racing. A hundred thoughts were running through his mind and he was starting to get a headache. Actually the option of keeping on the run and changing jobs every few months sounded pretty good to him right now. He just didn't like the idea of being under the government's thumb with the Witness Protection option. He could take off right now, but it probably wouldn't take the FBI long to track his car and him down again.

He was supposed to meet with Chief Travis that

evening to trade stamps and work on their albums. He'd have to tell the chief some kind of story if he wasn't going to be there. He didn't like the idea of lying to the chief, either. Alex had come to admire and respect Chief Travis. He seemed the kind of guy who would help, if he could, and a person you could trust. *I wonder what advice Chief Travis would give me.* He sat in his car for a while longer and finally decided to go ahead and meet with Travis that evening. He hadn't decided if he'd tell him about his dilemma and seek his advice or not. He'd have to think about it some more. He started his car and headed for his apartment.

When the two Soviet Embassy agents arrived at the Dallas-Ft.Worth Airport, they didn't see the FBI Special Agents posing as custodians and travelers waiting for flights. The agents spotted the pair of Russians when they entered the terminal. There were FBI surveillance teams outside and one agent posed as a customer in a rental car booth next to Hertz, the company the KGB always used for renting cars.

The FBI watched as the Soviets got to their rental and

then followed them all the way to Lake City, Texas. Arriving about 10 p.m., the two Soviets stopped at the Lake City Motel. They were observed taking two small bags from the rental car and entering room seven. They never left the room all night.

When Jim Travis got home from work, Abby met him at the door by throwing her arms around his neck and planting a long, sensual kiss on his lips. *What had come over her?* This was a kiss with a life of its own and was full of sexual intentions to Jim.

She finally pulled away from the kiss and looking into his eyes, said, "Jim, I'm sorry. I've been acting like a child." He put his arms around her and pulled her close to his body.

"I'm sorry, too, Abby," and they kissed again. This time it was not a long kiss, because he took her by the hand and started for the bedroom. They kissed and fondled each other and upon reaching the bedroom, each tore at removing their clothes, as if it was a race.

The night clerk at the Lake City Motel, Rex Tibbets,

worked the 4 to midnight shift every week day and as a stocking clerk at Dollar General on weekends. He was suspicious of the two foreigners who checked in earlier. Something one of the men said to the other, in their native tongue, sounded like Russian to him, but he couldn't be sure. He thought about calling Whimpy Davis. Tibbets had gotten to know Whimpy at Dollar General and knew his girlfriend was a police officer. Rex decided to call Whimpy.

"Hey man, waz up?" he answered.

"Sorry to bother you this late, Whimpy, but wanted to ask your wife about a couple of guys who checked in here at the motel."

"Oh, no problem, man, weez just sitting here watchin TV, hang on."

"Hello," said Hattie," who is this?" she asked in a stern tone.

"A, hi, a, my name is Rex and I work with Whimpy, or I, a, mean, Ray at Dollar General."

"Yes," responded Hattie.

"Well, ah, I also work some nights here at the Lake City

Motel and, well, two guys checked into the motel tonight and I think they may be Russians or something. I put them in room seven."

"What do you want me to do about it?" said Hattie, impatiently.

Tibbets answered, "It just seemed rather odd. They asked directions to the elevator in town and cripes sake, everyone knows where the elevator is, you can't miss it."

"Okay, I'll call the Chief and tell him of your concern."

"Oh, okay, thanks," and he heard Hattie hang up the receiver.

CHAPTER 44

Alex Nicola arrived at Jim Travis's trailer a few minutes before 8 p.m. He had his stamp albums in plastic grocery bags and Travis could tell immediately something was wrong. Alex had not decided if he would tell Travis about his true identity or not. He still hadn't decided even as he knocked on Travis's door. Inside, he looked around and asked, "Is Abby here?"

"No," said Travis. "She's spending the evening at my mom's place learning how to make a strawberry-rhubarb pie." Travis asked him how the job was going. Alex looked down at his feet.

Before he could answer, Travis asked him, "Jimmy, is everything okay?"

Alex looked up into Travis's eyes and said, "Jim, my name really isn't Jimmy Smith and my life is in danger."

For the next two hours, Alexander Nicola, told Jim Travis the whole story. He told about his family being murdered; stealing his friend, James Alan Smith's identity and his car; the FBI and Russians tracking him down in Beckley, West Virginia; and on and on. Travis would occasionally ask him a question, and Alex told him everything. He expressed his concern about the Witness Protection Program and was afraid the Russians might find him anyway. Travis listened intently to the story. Some ideas and options were starting to run through his mind. None of them were too good, however.

Travis's phone rang. He looked at the clock on the wall. It was 10:25 p.m. He hesitated to answer, for some reason, but finally did and recognized Hattie's voice. She explained to him the call she got from the motel clerk. Then she added Whimpy assured her Rex was a smart, level headed guy. She told Travis she considered not calling him, but decided to anyway, not knowing if it was important or not. Travis thanked her for the call and hung up the phone. He looked up to see Alex staring at him and immediately a plan started to form in Jim Travis's head.

As Travis explained his plan to Alex, Abby arrived and Travis had her join them. He quickly explained Alex's situation to her. She pulled up a chair with a heightened interest and a serious look on her face. The plan was to call Harley. Have him hide Alex's Impala in his garage for a few days. Alex would stay at Travis's trailer, out of sight, until the Feds and Russians gave up and left town. The only ones in on the plan would be Travis, Abby and Harley. If anyone asked, they would say Jimmy Smith must have left Lake City during the night and they had no idea where he was headed.

Alex agreed to the plan and Travis called Harley. He was sleeping but after hearing about Alex and his problem, he told them to meet him at the garage in 20 minutes. It was shortly after midnight before Travis and Alex got back to Travis's trailer. The Impala was safely hidden under an old tarp in one corner of the shop area which wasn't being used. On the way back from Harley's Auto Repair, they stopped at Alex's apartment where he quickly threw some of his things together into an old suitcase.

Back at Travis's trailer, Abby was waiting in the kitchen drinking a cup of coffee. Travis and Alex joined her at the table. It was then Abby brought up sleeping arrangements. "Jim, Alex can sleep on the sofa tonight, and I guess you and I can sleep in your room." Travis looked up quickly. With all the planning going on, he hadn't thought about who was going to sleep where.

He reluctantly nodded, adding, "I guess that would be okay," and glancing at Abby, saw maybe a slight gleam in her eye? However, that night they both kept to their respective sides of the bed, but Abby had some romantic thoughts as she drifted off to sleep.

CHAPTER 45

The next day Chief Travis got a call from the owner of Alex's apartment. He'd been called by the elevator manager who was concerned since Alex hadn't shown up for work. The manager went into Alex's apartment and saw that most of his things were gone and decided to call the police and report a missing person. Travis thanked him for the call and said he'd relay the information to the other officers.

It was at that time he called a meeting of Woody, Hattie and Val and told them Jimmy Smith did not shown up for work and the elevator manager and the owner of Jimmy's apartment were concerned. He asked them to let him know if they saw Jimmy or his car. He hated not telling them the whole truth, but maybe that would come later.

When Alex didn't show up at the elevator parking lot at 8 a.m. that morning, Emerson and Brewer scoured the parking lot looking for the 1972 Impala. They didn't find it. After some discussion, Emerson decided to make a call to the elevator and ask for Jimmy Smith. If asked, he would say he was Jimmy's uncle and needed to talk to him about a death in the family.

The girl answering the elevator phone put the call through to the manager. He stated Jimmy didn't show up for work that morning and he had contacted the owner of his apartment to see if his alarm clock maybe hadn't gone off. He hadn't heard back from the apartment owner. He gave Emerson the address of the apartment and the phone number of the owner. Before hanging up he offered his condolences about the family death.

Observing the FBI Agents waiting in the elevator

parking lot, the two Russians decided to stay put. They were parked mostly out of sight, behind a large 4-wheel drive pickup. They were going to let the FBI lead them to Alex. When the FBI car left the elevator lot, the Russians followed. The FBI pulled into a parking lot beside a Dairy Queen. They drove around to the back and pulled up to a pay phone booth.

An agent got out of his car and made a call. After the call, he got back into his car and he and his partner headed into the main part of town. The Russians kept well behind the FBI and actually lost them for a few blocks. A few minutes later, they were able to spot them again as the FBI vehicle pulled into an alley. The alley was behind the Jalapeno Café and the Soviets observed several cars parked behind the café.

Agents Emerson and Brewer did not see Alex's car among those parked behind his apartment house. The apartments were apparently above the café and another business that was closed. They decided to not contact the apartment owner but drive around town to see if they could spot the Impala. The Russians followed. After several hours, Emerson decided to call off the search and try to contact the apartment owner. He called the number the elevator manager gave him. When the apartment owner answered, he told Emerson it looked like Jimmy Smith abandoned his apartment. He also advised the agents he was concerned about the boy and notified the police.

Emerson put in a call to his supervisor in Washington, D.C. and after some discussion was told to spend the night and look some more in the morning. If the elevator manager had still not heard from Alex, they were to go back to Dallas to await further instructions. Emerson and Brewer got a room at the Lake City Motel, posing as IRS Agents. They were given room six.

CHAPTER 46

Alex watched TV all day inside Jim Travis's trailer. Abby was out running some errands. At one point during the day, he thought he heard something outside the trailer. He slowly opened the drapes and saw a young woman across the street bending over tending to some flowers. He recalled meeting her one day when she stopped by Harley's garage. As he was admiring her well-shaped body, she instantly looked up right at him. Alex quickly shut the drapes. He didn't move. *What if she saw him? What if she comes to the door? He couldn't answer it.*

About that time, Abby drove into one of the two parking spots in front of Jim's trailer. He sneaked another peek out through the drapes. He saw the young woman waving toward Abby and saying something. Abby waved back and said something back to the woman. Alex sat back down in front of the TV. When Abby came in she didn't say anything about the woman and started putting some groceries away.

Having lost the FBI several times as they drove around the town of Lake City, the KGB Agents finally decided to give up for the day and headed for a liquor store. When they returned to the Lake City Motel, they saw the FBI car parked in front of their motel room, room seven. They drove right by the motel and headed for the pay phone at the rear of the Dairy Queen. As they circled the building, someone was just exiting the phone booth. They waited until the person drove away and then placed a call to their embassy. They were instructed to spend another night and if Alex or his car were not spotted by the afternoon, they were to return to Washington. They drove to Gun Barrel

City and rented a room at a downtown hotel.

That evening, Abby fixed beef stroganoff and a strawberry-rhubarb pie for dinner. Before dinner, Travis had his usual brandy Manhattan, Abby had a glass of chardonnay and Alex had a Dr. Pepper. The conversation was limited but Travis did tell Alex about the elevator manager's concern and the apartment owner requesting a "Missing Persons," alert. Travis had given some thought about driving around a little that day hoping to spot the Russians or the FBI but nixed the idea.

The dinner was delicious and the pie was as good, or better, than Travis's mother made. Abby retired early, saying she was going to read and Travis and Alex watched the Carol Burnett Show. When Travis got into bed, he thought Abby was asleep, but he soon found out differently. When they started hearing Alex making some, slow, steady breathing sounds, Abby rolled on top of Jim and they celebrated their sharing a bed together once again.

The next day didn't go well both for the FBI or the KGB. They didn't see Alex or his car but did keep spotting each other's vehicles. Both tried to act like they were just a couple of salesmen looking for a coffee shop. The Russian agents were getting bored and started nipping on a bottle of Stolichnaya vodka. Finally, about mid-afternoon, having spotted the Soviets again that day for about the 4th time, Agent Brewer couldn't resist and he gave the KGB Agent the finger.

The Russian in the KGB car held up both fingers of both of his hands at Brewer. "That son of a bitch," exclaimed Brewer as he started to reach for his gun.

Emerson grabbed his arm and said, "Hey, hey. What the hell are you doing? You want to get us both fired and cause an international incident?" Brewer sat back in his seat and Emerson decided it was time to call off the search and head for Dallas.

The KGB driver took the wrong highway out of Lake City and before he realized it he ended up in Paris, Texas. They decided to drive to Little Rock and catch a plane there back to Washington, D.C. Just outside of Little Rock the Stolichnaya bottle was near empty and the driver was having a little trouble keeping the car between the lines. An Arkansas Highway Patrolman saw the swerving car, pulled it over and arrested both of the Russians: the driver for Driving Under the Influence and the passenger for Public Intoxication.

Several days later, after the embassy paid their fine, they were ordered to catch the next available flight from Little Rock to Moscow. Upon arrival, they were met by a KGB official and were informed their services were no longer needed. A few months later both were working at a Stolichnaya distillery outside of Moscow where the workers got to drink vodka during breaks and at lunch.

Major General Boris Kerensky's fate was sealed when Moscow found out about the two agents' arrest in Arkansas, and Alex Nicola had again gotten away. He was ordered back to Moscow, demoted to the rank of Colonel and put on administrative leave. Two months later he was given the responsibility of overseeing all the custodians assigned to the Kremlin with a small, one desk office, in one corner of the basement of the building.

Alex Nicola stayed with Jim and Abby for three more days. No one heard or saw anything more of the FBI or the KGB in Lake City. Alex decided to leave Lake City just in case someone decided to come back looking for him. He worked out the details with Harley and Jim to get his car out of the garage late one night and leave town. Between Harley and Travis they gave him $250. He thanked them and said he'd send them the money when he got the chance. They told him to forget it.

CHAPTER 47

Approximately seven months later, two babies were born, on the same day, at the Lake City Hospital. Hattie gave birth to a ten pound, two once boy and named him Raymond Charles Owens II. Whimpy was in seventh heaven, that is, until he had to go to the emergency room when a cigar ash got into one of his eyes.

Shirley Denson also had a boy. He weighed six pounds, five ounces and they named him Dale Evans Denson. Both delivered by Dr. Joseph Martin, who after delivering the Denson baby, cancelled all of his appointments and took two weeks off to recuperate.

Gladys Travis was delighted to hear of the two new births. She longed for grandchildren of her own, but knew that probably wasn't going to happen so she started baby quilts for the new arrivals.

Piotr Blok was promoted to the rank of Major General. He was put in charge of the Russian Embassy in Washington, as "Director of Public Affairs," Boris Kerensky's former position. Gagari Putin did marry Anna Burkhart and a few months later she quit her job with the Social Security Administration to stay home and start a family. Anton Pavlovich, the KGB Commander in Moscow was diagnosed with cirrhosis of the liver and died two months later.

The FBI Foreign Intelligence Supervisor at the Washington Field Office closed the file on Alexander Nicola. Agents Emerson and Brewer went back to their regular assignments of conducting foreign intelligence investigations. Emerson never forgot Alex Nicola and vowed to someday write a book about him, the death of his family and the "shadow of murder" that haunted the boy.

Of all the people in Lake City who got to know Alex, probably the person who would miss him the most was Harley Andrews. He had grown fond of the boy and treated him almost as if he was his son. He thought about asking him to keep in touch, but decided against it, figuring it might put a guilt trip on the boy and also cause him to worry about someone finding him. He also missed his help around the garage and told himself to keep his eye out for someone to help after school hours.

Jim Travis's relationship with his ex-wife, Abigal, blossomed. Abby started searching flea markets in the area buying up used books. After a few months, she quit her job at Dollar General and opened a used book store next to the Jalapeno Café.

Travis started doing some fishing with his old friend Harley. The weather had turned a little cooler and the fish were biting. He was spending more of his evenings with his stamp collection, especially when Abby was busy reading or watching TV. For some unknown reasons, Abby had drifted away from her previously obsessive interests in psychic and paranormal phenomenon. She found she liked to read romance novels and spend more of her leisure time trying new recipes. All this was fine with Jim Travis.

A month after the file was closed, the FBI received information from their El Paso, Texas Office that a 1972 Chevrolet Impala, registered to James Alan Smith and been found abandoned in a public parking lot just outside the border crossing into Ciudad Juarez. Agent Emerson asked US Customs and Immigration and Naturalization to check their records for James Alan Smith leaving the United States but they found no such record.

Had Alex actually slipped into Mexico undetected? Maybe he decided to do what the FBI suggested, work a few months and then move on. Would he have kept using the ID of James Alan Smith, or was he using a different name? Did he change his appearance? Maybe he had a wig, or was wearing his hair cut short. Perhaps he got a tattoo or maybe a nose ring. Or, he may have just settled in somewhere and now works at the local Wal-Mart. How does one continue to exist, always looking over his shoulder and trying to keep out of, "murder's shadow"? Only Alexander Nicola knows the answers to these questions. Or does he?

The End